Books by A. H. Lee

The Incubus Series
Incubus Caged
Incubus Bonded
Incubus Dreaming
Burn - a Prequel Story

The Knight and the Necromancer
The Capital
The Border
The Sea

Incubus Dreaming

The Incubus Series Book 3

by A. H. Lee

Pavonine Books 2017

© 2017 A. H. Lee
Cover Art by Starla Huchton
A product of Pavonine Books

All rights reserved to the author. This material may not be reproduced, modified, or distributed without the express prior permission of the copyright holder. For more information, email abigail.hilton@gmail.com.

For Alesa. I'm so sorry you'll never read this.

Special thanks to Amy, who wanted more for Jessica.

Special thanks to Nobilis, who wanted more for Lucy.

1

Azrael

Laurence Nigel Crowley—Ren to his friends and Lord Azrael to everyone else—woke in an enormous, downy bed, covered in equal parts panther and books. Morning sunlight shone from a picture frame that covered most of one wall. It was an enchantment, since there were no actual windows in this bedroom, but the view overlooking the palace gardens was real enough—dewy and soft with dawn mist.

A naked young woman lay nestled under the covers against one of Azrael's shoulders, leafing through a novel. Azrael smiled sleepily and whispered, "That one has a nice hot spring."

Jessica's blue eyes flicked up, crinkling with pleasure. Her honey blond hair fell in a messy halo around her shoulders. "I like the scene with the minnows," she whispered back. "And the food sounds amazing. Does it actually taste good?"

Azrael nodded. Or he tried to. Mal's chin and head were pressed against his face on the opposite side. One massive, velvet paw lay across his chest. Jessica rested the book across her stomach and sighed. "Oh, I don't know. You always pick out good places. The last one I picked was a disaster."

"It was more exercise than I expected."

"How was I supposed to know the cows were carnivorous? If the author does not mention it in the next book, I will send a strongly worded letter."

They spent most of their dates in the pocket worlds of various novels, created by the books' proximity to Azrael's collection of grimoires. Azrael extricated his arm from behind Jessica to rub his eyes. "Spoiler alert."

"You pick."

"It's your turn!"

Jessica shrugged. She reached across him and snagged another volume. "I don't want to go wandering around in this one, but we should definitely read it. I think Mal would like it, too. There are talking cats. Er. Cat creatures, anyway."

Azrael blinked at the book. He was still getting used to having someone in his life who liked books as much as he did. "That's one of the new batch, isn't it?" His agents went all over the kingdoms collecting literature for him—everything from rare magical texts to novels and cookbooks.

Jessica nodded. "I picked it up off the kitchen table; was that alright?"

"Of course. There were a few magical odds and ends in that pile, but I don't bring anything very powerful into my suite. That one's just a novel."

Mal finally stirred against his shoulder. Azrael could remember a time when his pet demon would have woken at the creak of a board, the brush of a whisker, the softest of muttered commands. But not since he'd returned from his four-month vacation. Not since he'd moved into Azrael's bed. Lately, Mal slept deeply and woke up purring.

He raised his head at last and gave a toothy yawn, pink tongue curling. He was lying on top of the sheets, while Azrael and Jessica were under them. He flopped all the way across Azrael onto Jessica and licked her face, his purr vibrating through both their bodies.

Jessica gave a squawk that ended in a giggle and caught his head in both hands. "Good morning to you, too, silly."

Azrael raised the arm that had been under Mal and flexed his fingers with a grimace. "My hand is asleep."

Mal promptly switched to snuffling and licking around Azrael's face and neck, which tickled tremendously and made him gasp with laughter. Mal squirmed all the way across Azrael and flopped over onto his back between them, scattering books and displacing pillows. Jessica rubbed his belly. "You are ridiculous."

Mal purred louder.

"I am going for a swim with Yuli this morning," continued Jessica. "I need to leave in about five minutes."

Mal opened one gem-green eye. "What?" He shifted into a man with a ripple of black smoke, his green eyes hardly changing, his black curls a glorious mess. "Stay and cuddle with us."

Jessica kissed his nose. "Later."

"When later?"

Jessica laughed. "Tomorrow? Tonight? This afternoon—!" She broke off as Mal ran his fingers from her shoulder, down over a breast. He circled a nipple and then drifted lower, pushing the sheets down as he went. He exposed her stomach with its new contours of muscle—a product of her devotion to her sword practice.

Azrael's natural inclination was towards men, but he'd spent so many years in isolation that the ability to touch or confide in anyone felt like a gift. He'd spent the two decades since he summoned Mal trying desperately to maintain emotional space between himself and the incubus he loved, but who had, until recently, been a constant threat to his life. Jessica was a breath of fresh air—more human than Mal, deeply intuitive, and willing to be patient with the complexities of their relationship. She was a lovely creature, no matter one's tastes, and Azrael enjoyed seeing her and Mal together. Most importantly, she was his friend.

"Mal, if she needs to leave, let her leave."

Mal spoke in a voice full of confidence and mischief. "Five minutes?"

"Mal…" groaned Jessica.

"Four? Three? Give me three minutes."

Jessica drew a long breath. "Well, I suppose," she said with mock-gravity.

Mal straddled her briefly, then settled down on the other side, putting Jessica between them. He wasn't using magic at all. Mal did love a challenge. He caught one of Jessica's hands over her head and twined their fingers together. His other hand made circles down her body, pushing the sheet farther and farther. Azrael could tell that Jessica had expected him to go under the sheet, not push it off, and her face went a little pink when he exposed the blond curls at her crotch and then flipped the entire sheet off.

Azrael started to reach for a book—not because he was bored, but out of habit, because this was how he'd always distracted himself when Mal was feeding. Mal's green eyes flicked up and he murmured. "Don't do that. Watch. She likes it when you watch."

Jessica's flush deepened. "Mal…"

Mal looked down at her, his smirk tempered with affection. "It makes her a little embarrassed and very wet."

Jessica was flushed all the way to her nipples now and Mal drew a delicate line back and forth over her belly, refusing to go lower. Azrael was starting to feel a little pink himself. He was the only person still covered in blankets. Mal grinned at him from under his long, dark lashes. "Touch her and see."

"Mal," growled Jessica. "This was your idea."

"Hmm-hmm." His hand moved back up, cupping a breast. Jessica gave a little impatient kick. Mal's tongue glided over a nipple and then up to her throat. "Ask him to touch you."

Jessica was breathing deeply. Her eyes flicked desperately to Azrael. "You want to p-play?" She broke off in a yelp as Mal nibbled.

"One minute left," murmured Mal against her neck. "Or we send you off to swimming lessons so frustrated you'll end up eating some poor courtier on your way."

"I am not going for l-lessons," choked Jessica.

Azrael had touched Jessica before. Hells, she'd climbed onto his cock before. He'd just never done it quite this unsupervised. Hesitantly, he reached down to the sensitive skin behind Jessica's knee, touching her as he would a nervous horse. He trailed his fingers all the way up her thigh, watching her chest and belly rise and fall more rapidly, until he slid two fingers inside her.

Mal was kissing her on the mouth now, and she gave a muffled mew. "You like that?" murmured Mal. "You like his fingers inside of you? He's watching you. Every bit of you. And gods, you're pretty, Jessica."

She *was* wet. Azrael tried to make sense of all the slippery, muscular warmth. He wasn't sure what he was feeling for, but she didn't seem to mind his stroking. Mal moved his hand back down her body and curled around Azrael's fingers, guiding them to a rough, feathery something further inside. Jessica gasped and pressed her body hard against his hand. Azrael's thumb found her clit. That, he could actually *see*—pink and glistening between her dark blond curls.

Mal's hands were running everywhere else—her face, her back, her breasts, almost rough. Jessica panted, bucked against Azrael's hand. "He's awfully good with those hands," purred Mal. "And you know I love you, or I'd never share him."

A little too honest, Mal, thought Azrael.

Jessica must have thought so, too, because her body stilled for a moment. Mal leaned close to her ear and murmured. "We should share you at the Revels in front of everyone."

That did it. Her body clenched around Azrael's fingers, his thumb still stroking. She buried her face against Mal's shoulder, her breath coming hard and fast. An instant later, she fell back panting against the pillows, then promptly scrambled up and dragged them into a hug. "I love you both." She caught her breath in a dramatic pause. "But that was six minutes."

Azrael barked a laugh.

Mal made a face. "Oh, but you were having fun!"

Jessica sprang from the bed, staggered, got her balance. "I need to go!"

Mal shouted after her, "Swimming is not as fun as we are!"

"I can do both!" shot Jessica over her shoulder as she darted into the washroom.

2

Azrael

Mal flopped back down, dark curls tangling over the pillow, always impossibly clean. Azrael sat up and reached for a tissue from the bedside table to wipe his hand. "I need to talk to my staff this morning. The first of the guests will be arriving next week."

"I still can't believe we're letting those people wander around our territory," grumbled Mal.

Azrael had to agree. If anyone had told him a year ago that he would invite the High Mage Council to tour the Shrouded Isle, he would have told them to recalibrate their scrying pool. Of course, if they'd told him that he would wake up naked in bed with Mal and a woman, he would have said they'd lost their minds.

But seven months ago, Jessica had walked into their lives and everything had changed. Now, Azrael was seriously considering Lord Loudain's suggestion that he host a school here, and it was only natural that the families of future students wanted the Council's blessing. It was a gesture of goodwill towards other magicians—something that Azrael had long disdained. He was feeling strangely generous these days.

Mal smiled abruptly. "There's a Revel this evening for the courtiers. I'd forgotten."

"Yes, I want you fed," said Azrael. "In case there's any trouble with 'those people' we're letting onto our island. So don't just mess about with Jessica." He felt the latter admonishment necessary because Mal had shown an alarming reluctance to feed directly of late.

Mal yawned. "I'll soak up plenty of energy just being there."

Azrael paused in stacking the scattered books on the bedside table. He gave Mal an arch look. "What do you call a monogamous incubus?"

Mal sputtered.

"Hungry," said Azrael. "And weak."

Mal rolled over and dragged him down into the bed. "Weak? Really?" He was a wall of muscle and warm skin, his thigh sliding across Azrael's legs, one big warm hand on his chest. The other arm slid behind his head. "You want to wrestle and see who wins?"

Haven't we been doing that for twenty years? Azrael laughed against his mouth. "You know what I mean—" He caught his breath as Mal nuzzled under his chin and kissed his way to the pulse of his throat. With an effort, Azrael formed words. "We can't…can't even do this if you're hungry."

"I know," said Mal. "I won't be." He pulled back, his green eyes electric and inches from Azrael's face. "Come to the Revels with us."

Azrael gave a shaky laugh. He was uncomfortably aware of his own arousal and wished Mal would just kiss him again.

"I'm serious," said Mal. "Come with us."

"Feeding on me will not accomplish anything, either."

Mal rolled his eyes. "I don't mean to feed."

Azrael blinked at him. "I'll be in my viewing box…"

"Reading." Mal said the word with more contempt than Azrael thought necessary. He made up for it by moving his hand down to stroke Azrael's cock. Azrael's eyes snapped shut. It was still so startling to be touched casually in bed. Mal kissed him on the mouth and murmured, "You love dressing us up like dolls. Dress yourself up this time. Come play games with us and talk to people and drink enough to feel tipsy and dance! Let me dance with you, Ren. Let me pour magic into you with all that energy washing around us. Please?"

Azrael swallowed. "That sounds…"

"Fun. It sounds fun."

"It sounds dangerous." There were still very few people who knew the extent of Azrael's relationship with Mal and Jessica. A sorcerer sleeping with demons might be considered too dangerous to live by plenty of people in the magical community. "Not when we're about to host the High Mage Council."

Mal looked disappointed, although his hand kept up a distracting caress under the blankets. "Another time?"

"Maybe."

Mal grinned. "And then I can throw you in the pool with all your clothes on and carry you off to bed when you're too tired to stand up anymore."

Azrael shook with laughter. "This is a rather specific fantasy."

"Mmm." Mal moved over, completely on top of him, his forearms cradling Azrael's head. Azrael gasped at the sudden weight and the pressure of Mal's cock against his. "I love waking up on top of you," whispered Mal.

Azrael snorted a laugh. "You also love going to sleep on top of me!"

"Did I really hurt your hand?"

"No."

"You said it hurt."

"Worth it."

Mal kissed him. Azrael slid his arms around Mal's neck, wrapped his legs around his waist and gave himself up to the pleasure of their naked bodies moving against each other, the heat of his lover's mouth, the artistry of his powerful shoulders, and the dense softness of his hair.

When Azrael was breathing hard, Mal paused to slide a pillow under his hips. They'd found a spell for lubrication—ridiculously simple, but Mal was a source of magic, not a user, so

Azrael had to say the word himself while running his hand over Mal's cock. Mal pulled back to let him do it, his eyes blinking shut. "I want to take down your wards," he whispered.

Azrael paused. Mal had been doing that a lot lately. He'd figured out how to unpick Azrael's wards, but he wouldn't do it without permission. Mal was a powerful astral demon, intimately acquainted with Azrael's magic and his personal style. It was not surprising that he'd found a way inside the wards. Azrael knew he should restructure them, make it impossible for anyone to take them down except himself. But somehow he hadn't gotten around to it.

"Yes," he whispered, and Mal's fingers immediately danced over the skin of his cheek, flipping and twisting invisible strands of magic, brushing his lips and nose. Azrael's wards lit up automatically at this intrusion. Mal raised his fingers. Twisting lines of blue light spread from them like plucked spider web, stretching…

Snap!

Azrael felt the shock over his entire body as Mal breached his wards. And then there was no space between them at all. Mal was in his head and everywhere else, pulling on his magic, the warmth unspooling through Azrael in a dizzy rush. Mal's cock pressed inside him, hitting just the right spot—a gentle nudge at first, almost unbearably exquisite as he picked up speed.

Azrael whimpered and curled against him, wrapping his legs more tightly around his waist, panting and trembling. He wanted to do this and nothing else forever. He wanted it to end at once because it was too much, too much, too much. He wanted…wanted…

The orgasm hit him with blinding force, wrung him out, and left him shuddering. Mal murmured against his ear, "This is what you want. To feel this helpless. And this safe."

Azrael couldn't deny it. Not with an incubus reading his desires as plainly as Azrael could read a textbook. Mal's cock was still inside him, and there was still a thread of energy humming between them. *Any other demon with his summoner unwarded and flat on his back would just eat me up.* "Mal you are so special," the words slipped out before he really thought about them. "And I love you so much."

Mal trembled. He pressed himself deep inside and finished with a flood of pleasure that communicated itself in a strange echo down their shared connection. The thread of feeding eased and then ceased. *One day, he may not stop,* thought Azrael. It was a risk he took each time he allowed this to happen.

Mal pulled back, watching his face. "What are you thinking?" Mal could read sexual desire like a musician with perfect pitch, but he could not actually read minds, and other emotions were often confusing to him.

Azrael raised a hand to Mal's cheek. "That I wouldn't change a thing." *And maybe there will come a time for public dancing.*

3

Mal

Mal had a habit of turning back into a panther after sex. It just seemed like a cuddlier shape, although he'd taught himself not to knead people with his claws. Bleeding did not make people feel cuddly. He contented himself with licking Azrael all over until he begged to be let up. Then Mal bounded around the room while Azrael put his wards back together. He waited impatiently while his master took a shower and dressed. Mal noticed that Azrael had chosen riding clothes.

"Are we checking the perimeter today?"

"Yes, I thought it would be a good idea before people start arriving," said Azrael as he fastened his cuffs. He'd stopped at the bedside table, and Mal remembered that his collar was lying there. He'd been taking it off at night lately, but Azrael needed Mal's magic for things like checking perimeter wards.

Mal came over and waited for Azrael to drop it around his neck, but Azrael paused. Mal could tell he wanted to say something, but he couldn't seem to decide what. "Mal," he said at last, "would you mind if I took a link out of your collar?"

Mal frowned at him. "Why?"

"It's something for Jessica. I'd rather talk to her about it before I explain, but...would you mind?"

Mal shook his ears. "I guess not. It's *your* focus."

"But it's got your blood in it."

Mal flicked his tail. "It's made of blood and magic, Boss. Yours and mine. If the wrong person got hold of a link, they could hurt us a lot. Is that why you're asking me?"

"Yes."

Mal put his paws on the bed and reared up to lick Azrael's face. "I trust you. And Jessica. Do whatever you like with it."

Azrael nodded. He cradled the collar in his hands and said a word that vibrated in the air. The collar fell apart.

There'd been a time when Mal would have given anything to see that collar disintegrate. Now, it made him anxious. Azrael seemed to sense this and reached out to rub his ears before continuing.

Mal watched, fascinated, as Azrael carefully selected a single link, then spoke the spell again. The collar reformed, running together like mercury. Azrael slid the extra link into his pocket and held out the collar to Mal. "Let's go check the perimeter."

4

Jessica

Jessica hung suspended in the clear waters of a mountain spring, trying to see the details of an ancient tile floor below. Clouds of fish obscured her view, parted, obscured it again. They were teal and red and cream and orange—the same colors as the tiles. Jessica thought, although she could not be certain, that they changed color.

A girl swam by beneath her, naked as Jessica, her hair a shiny black ribbon in the clear water. Sunlight dappled on her strong arms and legs, kicking rhythmically. Jessica was reminded of the mermaids she'd once watched with Mal. But that had been in a pocket world inside a storybook. Yuli was real.

And even though she seemed preternaturally aquatic, even Yuli eventually had to breathe. She turned abruptly towards the surface and kicked upward. Jessica popped up along with her. Sound came back into the world—a flood of birdsong, the babble of the river and the nearby waterfall.

Jessica and Yuli gasped and grinned at each other in the misty spray of the falls, wet hair plastered to their heads. "I think it's a bathhouse!" exclaimed Yuli.

"Oh!" Jessica had been thinking summer cottage, but maybe that was because she'd just come from one. "That makes sense."

"That long part with no tilework is one of the pools," said Yuli. "Also…you couldn't see it from up there, but if you dive low enough to see through the fallen arch, there's a statue inside…" She grinned. "Of two gentlemen, um, *bathing* each other."

Jessica waggled her eyebrows. "Really?"

Yuli backstroked away from her. "Yes, they're very devoted to cleanliness."

"I need more details!"

"Then you'll have to swim down."

"That is not fair, Yuli!"

Jessica considered trying to dive to the statue, but she didn't think she could do it without a rest, so she paddled to the bank. "I'm still teaching you to swim," said Yuli behind her.

"I'm taught!" proclaimed Jessica, hoisting herself out of the water onto a rock, just barely warm from the mid-morning sun. She selected a towel from the pile they'd brought, and pulled it around her shoulders. Her body had the pleasant ache of early morning exercise. The air smelled of earth and the faintly mineral odor of the spring. The water bubbling out of the deep section was quite warm, although it mingled with the cooler water churning down from the falls.

Yuli popped up beside the rock, moisture beading on her nut-brown skin and the swell of her breasts. "I would die of shame if you told anyone that I taught you to swim while you were dog paddling."

She gave Jessica's foot a playful tug as though to pull her in, but Jessica resisted. "I want to sit here a moment. Come sit with me."

Yuli relented and clambered, dripping, onto the rock. She grabbed a towel to wipe her face, then a handful of nuts from their daypack. "I'm glad we found this place."

"Me, too."

Jessica turned away from the vision of the pool and waterfall—one of a series that tumbled from the bluffs on the highest side of the island. From up here, she could see where the water gurgled through wheat fields and on into the gardens around

Azrael's palace. It was all part of the Rapunzel—a river that wound like a silver braid through the Shrouded Isle.

Jessica and Yuli had followed the river through the gardens and off the palace grounds on horseback a week ago, looking for the waterfalls. They'd been delighted to find a grotto pool, clear as glass, with fish in the strangest colors and drowned ruins at the bottom.

"Just be careful," Azrael had told Jessica. "I've worked hard to make this island safe, but we are surrounded by the Shattered Sea, and things change fast this close to the source."

The "source" he referred to was magic itself—raw potential that bubbled out of the Shattered Sea for reasons even the world's most powerful sorcerer did not understand. Nobody had ever learned how to distill magic from the waves, but all innate magic was stronger here, and the world was thinner.

The Shrouded Isle had been held by a malevolent naiad and other monsters before Azrael. He'd been the first human to take back the island since the Sundering. Remnants of a forgotten, pre-sundering kingdom still existed on the island—a kingdom that was mostly below the waves now, eaten by the sea during that cataclysm when magic had overwhelmed everything. The inhabitants of that lost kingdom had obviously used magic, but it had been tamer back then.

Jessica had grown up in the Provinces—the farthest from the Kingdoms of the Shattered Sea, just a step removed from the mundane world beyond. Magic worked unreliably in the Provinces. Jessica suspected that was part of the reason her succubus nature had lain dormant until she arrived on the Shrouded Isle.

Yuli, on the other hand, had grown up in the island kingdom of Caowah, next door to the Emerald Isles. People from her region were more accustomed to magical creatures and magical threats, but that didn't slow them down. They even kayaked and swam in the Shattered Sea and boldly ate its fish. Yuli had killed a hydra with a knife once. She spoke of it as she might a shark.

She'd been Jessica's second friend here. Second after Tod, who was an entirely different sort of friend. Yuli loved books. She wrote novels, although she didn't show them to many people. When she'd received the invitation to go as tribute to the Shrouded Isle, she'd welcomed the adventure. She'd joyfully thrown herself into dance lessons, etiquette lessons, parties, clothes, and sexual adventures with powerful people. However, her plans for her own future had never changed. "I'm going to use the money from my time here to open a bookshop," she'd told Jessica. "Then I'm going to marry Terrance Pimbrook."

He was Yuli's boyfriend from back home, and she wrote to him every day. "The Shrouded Isle is kind of fake," she'd said to Jessica once. "I mean, it's amazing. But it exists to put powerful people in a frame of mind to be agreeable. I don't mind being part of it for a while, but I want a life in the real world."

In truth, the sexually charged atmosphere of the Shrouded Isle existed to feed Mal, who was the primary source of Azrael's magic. However, Yuli wasn't exactly wrong, either. Azrael's goal in life was to keep peace in the complex world of the Shattered Sea. There'd been times when he'd done this by questionable means, but his court certainly existed to put powerful people in a frame of mind to hear reason. Jessica supposed that, even if she hadn't gotten herself hopelessly entangled with Mal and Azrael, she wouldn't have minded being a part of that, either. For a while, at least.

Yuli hadn't said anything about Terrance since Jessica's return to the island. Jessica sensed that something had changed, but she felt she had no right to pry. She was keeping too many secrets herself.

Yuli did not approve of Mal. She rarely said anything about him, but when she did, she called him "creepy." Jessica didn't think Yuli knew what Mal was. She probably thought he'd come to the island as a courtier and stayed as one of Azrael's mysterious hangers-on. Jessica was sure Yuli had made no connection between the panther who often paced at Azrael's side and the big, dark-haired man who showed up at the Revels and who had fallen into Jessica's bed. However, Jessica doubted that telling Yuli the truth would improve her opinion of Mal. She was even a little afraid that telling Yuli the truth about herself might end their friendship.

People living in the islands of the Shattered Sea had little patience with monsters. Tod, after all, had nearly lost his life there when he'd been bitten by a werewolf as a child. It wasn't his fault, but that hadn't stopped his family from exiling him to Azrael's court to prevent his likely execution. Jessica had gotten the idea that Yuli was more open-minded than most people in the island kingdoms, but that didn't mean she would be able to accept Jessica as a succubus who was in a triad relationship with an incubus and a sorcerer.

Yuli shoved her own towel under her butt to make the rock more comfortable and stared at the beautiful view, impervious to her nudity. "It's nice to have you back, Jessica. Nobody else wants to do stuff like this with me."

Jessica smiled. "But…?"

Yuli looked at her in exasperation. "Alright, fine, I'll ask! *Why* did you come back? Did you marry that lunatic? I can't decide whether you're acting married."

Jessica burst out laughing. "I'm sorry. I'm not comfortable talking about some of it."

"Yes, well…" Yuli shivered and reached for another towel. The fall air was cool even if the water was warm. "It's your business; I know that. But you wrote me every week for a while and then you just sort of…stopped. I enjoyed hearing about all the places you visited. If you love that Mal fellow, I don't care. I thought he might be messing with you, but clearly he's serious. So, I admit I was wrong, and I'm sorry. Please tell me."

Jessica bit her lip. "Mal is…tied to the Shrouded Isle. To Azrael's work here. He wanted to come back, and after being gone for a few months, I did, too. We visited the Provinces. He met my family. But…it didn't feel like home anymore."

Yuli looked at her wide-eyed. "Are you going to live here permanently?"

That is a very good question. "I don't know, Yuli. I'm happy right now."

Yuli grinned. "Well, then, I'm happy for you."

"How's Terrance?" asked Jessica, trying to change the subject.

Yuli's expression did not alter, but that in itself was odd. Usually she lit up like a lightbulb when she talked about Terrance. "He's fine. Listen, I'm writing a story about carnivorous plants that take over the world, and a plucky band of children who save it. You visited the sentient forests of Karth, right? Tell me about them!"

5

Jessica

Two hours later, Yuli had to go to a language lesson. Jessica had planned to return with her, but changed her mind at the last minute. Jessica got dressed and hiked the rest of the way to the top of the ridge, where water bubbled out of a jumble of rocks. She followed a faint trail to a meadow that looked down onto the rocky beach on the less habitable side of the Shrouded Isle. To her amusement, she spotted Azrael and Mal in the distance—Azrael on horseback, Mal loping beside him as a panther.

The horse was Azrael's favorite—a ghost-gray mare with a beautiful, smooth gait. She paid no more attention to Mal than if he'd been a large dog. She was cantering in the surf, Azrael stopping now and then to run his fingers through the air. Arcs of blue light shot up whenever he did this, temporarily outlining a twisting net of spells that lay like a dome across the island. They were complex wards that protected the Shrouded Isle from incursion by magicians, other-worldly creatures, or any of the nameless horrors that might crawl or slither out of the Shattered Sea.

"They look happy to be home," said a friendly male voice behind Jessica.

She smiled. "I thought I spotted something in the trees. You shouldn't spy on girls skinny dipping, Tod. It's not polite."

"I averted my eyes!" he exclaimed. "*You* should not go skinny dipping in isolated parts of this island without someone standing watch. Do you have any idea what Azrael catches in those spell traps? What if something got through? No, don't turn around, please. Give me a moment to…change."

Jessica sighed. He'd never let her see his wolf form, which she thought was unfair. She'd seen all the rest of him. Tod was one of the few people she'd felt comfortable feeding on in the early days when her demonic nature began to manifest. He was more resilient than a normal human, harder to hurt because he was a werewolf. However, Tod's relationship with his animal form was very different from Mal's. To Tod, it was a curse that had separated him from his wizard family, wrecked his innate magical abilities, and prevented him from going home for more than short visits. He was not proud of it.

"I wouldn't judge," said Jessica quietly. "I'm a succubus for gods' sakes!"

Tod said nothing. Jessica had gotten the idea that the transformation hurt, although he'd never told her so. At last, he spoke again. "Alright, I'm good."

Jessica turned around. Tod was sitting on the grass, barefoot in his trousers. He'd put on a shirt, but hadn't buttoned it. His red hair looked a little wild. His pale, freckled skin showed stark against the grass. He had a sleek, lightly muscled build—deceptive, because he was very strong. His open shirt gave a tantalizing peak at the contours of his chest and stomach.

Jessica came to sit beside him. "Were you carrying those around in your mouth?" Unlike Mal, Tod could not make clothes from magic.

He gave an ironic smile and raised a bag on a string out of the grass. "Rolled up in there, around my neck. It works pretty well, although everything ends up wrinkled."

Jessica leaned against his shoulder. It felt good to be home. Below them, in the distance, Mal and Azrael had stopped to investigate something on the beach. Mal began digging, sending up a cataract of sand. "See," murmured Tod, "they've found one."

Jessica watched as Azrael jumped off the horse. The barrier behind him sparked and fizzled, sending out random flashes of blue light up over the dome and across the sand. Mal soon unearthed a jar about the size of a human head. "Is that a spirit vessel?" asked Jessica, craning her neck.

"Yep," said Tod, "a spell trap. And judging by the way Mal is acting, it has something in it."

Mal was behaving like a hunting dog on point. He'd backed away from the jar and stood rigid, tail twitching. He and Azrael were talking to each other, but Tod and Jessica were too far away to hear what they were saying. Azrael made a crushing motion with his hands, and the vessel shattered. Something bigger exploded into view, almost as though it had been under the sand the whole time. The thing looked like a young girl, naked and in distress, her arms reaching.

Jessica gasped. "What's wrong with her body?"

Her waist melded into a muscular, gray column. Then the rest of the creature flopped out of the sand, and the girl was just a stalk bobbing from its head—a meat puppet. The head beneath was fishy, massive, and full of teeth.

"It's like an angler fish," said Tod with interest.

Jessica clapped a hand over her mouth. "It's like a horrible monster! Gods, I'm going to dream about that."

"I wonder if it can make the lure talk," continued Tod amiably. "Help! Help! I'm drowning!"

"Tod!" exclaimed Jessica.

"Jessica! This is why you shouldn't go skinny dipping in the woods without someone on watch. There's a good reason nobody lived here until Azrael came along and locked it down with Mal's magic."

Below them, Mal was dancing around the creature that seemed disturbingly agile on its fins. The child—the lure—on its head bobbled and flopped grotesquely. Jessica could tell that Mal was trying to keep the monster's attention. Behind it, Azrael drew something out of his pocket—a weaponized spell, no doubt. He spoke to it, and then threw it onto the creature. The beast convulsed and shimmered with blue light. The great jaws went *snap, snap, snap!* Then it began to melt—first into a black ooze like tar, then, as Azrael continued to pour spells over the monster, into mud. Finally, the dissolving lump brightened into clear amber. In the end, the monster made a relatively small puddle. It lay on the sand in a discreet gobbet like mercury, unable to dissolve or mix with anything else.

It was ambrosia. Undifferentiated magic. Jessica suspected that turning such a monster into ambrosia had required a great deal of magical energy from Mal.

Her suspicions were confirmed when Mal flopped down onto the sand. He said something, probably a joke, because Azrael laughed. Then he whistled for the horse, who'd remained remarkably calm during all this. Azrael retrieved an object from his saddle bags—a vessel that siphoned up the ambrosia the instant Azrael touched it to the puddle.

He left the last bit, scooped it up, and held it out to Mal. Mal stood to lap the ambrosia out of Azrael's cupped hands. Then he raised his head the short distance to Azrael's face and licked him just as enthusiastically. Azrael jerked back, but he was laughing.

"There's something they wouldn't have done before," remarked Tod.

Jessica smiled. "They are so happy."

"I don't know if you realize how unusual that is."

"I've been told."

Tod glanced at her sidelong. "Do they really...? I mean, I know they *want* to, but *can* they...?"

"Fuck?" supplied Jessica. "Well, yes. Now that they've figured that out, Mal puts him to sleep with sex and wakes him up with sex and interrupts him with sex..."

Tod was shaking with laughter.

Jessica spread her hands. "And Azrael just...lets him! He was so lonely for so long..." She broke off. "You won't tell anyone I said that, will you? Azrael is really worried about people finding out."

"Of course not," said Tod. She knew she could trust him. She'd trusted him with bigger secrets. And besides, it was her life, too. She had to be able to talk to someone about it.

"And you're...happy in all this?"

Jessica waggled her eyebrows. "I am *involved* in all this."

Tod laughed again. "I can't imagine. In fact, I can't even imagine Azrael and Mal. I can't imagine Azrael and anyone!"

"He's shy and secretive," said Jessica more seriously. "Even if he hadn't summoned an incubus—if he hadn't been forced to stay celibate to control Mal—he might have ended up alone. But he's a dear creature...once you get past all those wards." She decided not to mention that Mal could take them down.

Tod shook his head, as though Azrael being a "dear creature" was also something he couldn't imagine. "Are you planning to stay on the Shrouded Isle permanently, Jessica?"

That question again. Jessica wrapped her arms around her knees, around the loose fabric of the trousers she'd worn for hiking. "I think so."

She caught Tod's smile out of the corner of her eyes and felt suddenly guilty. "Tod, am I...keeping you too busy? I mean..." *Am I keeping you from finding someone else? Someone who could give you more of herself than I can?*

"No," he said, "I just..." He curled a freckled toe in the grass. "The courtiers are so interesting and beautiful. But they leave after four years. I used to get kind of attached to some of them. When they left..." He shrugged. She could tell he was trying not to make a big deal out of something painful. "People say they'll write, but they eventually stop. I can't blame them. They remember this place like a dream. Most of the permanent residents are older than me. Some of the staff are my age, but I don't find real friends very often." He wasn't looking at her. He was trying to keep it light.

Jessica put an arm around his waist and squeezed. "Yes, I want to make my home here."

He gave a sigh of relief and hugged her back. "I don't need to be your one and only," he said into her hair. "We don't even need to fuck! I live on the Shrouded Isle. Sex is everywhere. But I...I so hoped you'd stay. And if you're hungry. *Ever* hungry."

Jessica pushed him back on the grass. They hadn't done this since she'd come home two weeks ago. It felt good to touch him again. "I missed you, too."

Tod brushed a hand over her face. "But Jessica, truly, are *they* what you want? I mean, I see that you've solved a problem for them, and the three of you are having fun right now. But... you told me once you want children."

Jessica stopped. She'd thought they were just going to have a welcome-home romp, but this was a more serious conversation. Her hair, still damp and braided to keep it out of the way, fell down across Tod's collar bone. The expression on her face must have looked like pain, because Tod said quickly, "We don't have to talk about it. I'm sorry. It's none of my business."

Jessica had been about to crawl on top of him. Instead, she settled down beside him and put her head on his chest. "No, it's a fair question." She took a deep breath. "I really love them. And I missed this place, Tod. It's hard to be a demon out in the world—harder than I thought. This is a good place for me and Mal. I want to make it work here, but you're right. I'm worried about that—about wanting kids. Maybe I have to give it up? I hope…I hope that doesn't make me bitter in the end. Right now, I'm so happy, but… I don't know."

Tod petted her hair. "Have you talked to them about it?"

"Not exactly. Mal and I can't have babies. You probably knew that. We can only have children with mortals. Azrael gave us infertility charms before we left. Mine is under my skin—pretty hard to get out, I imagine. Anyway, if Mal and I can't have babies, that leaves…"

Tod's breathing stuttered. "Oh, gods, Jessica." Tod sat up and stared at her. "He'll never say yes!"

"He does seem quite set against the idea of me 'making little demons,'" said Jessica gloomily, "with anyone."

"Let alone with *him!*" exploded Tod. "And if other magicians found out…? A sorcerer and a succubus? What if the kid is a demon who can use magic?"

"I know, I know," muttered Jessica. "I sort of…brought it up sideways at one point, and he was not receptive."

Tod's red-gold eyebrows drew together in concentration. "You should bring it up directly. Soon. Before you've spent years here with them."

"I know," muttered Jessica. "I'm just nervous, alright? This is so perfect right now. It's everything I wanted. Except…"

"Except in a few years, you're going to want to have kids, and by then, it'll be much harder to leave. Also, if Azrael doesn't want more demons in the world, if he knows that's why you're leaving… Jessica, he'll have you locked down so tightly by then…!"

Jessica screwed her eyes shut. "Don't say that. He wouldn't—" She bit her lip. *Wouldn't he?* An uncomfortable memory flashed through her head: Azrael calmly asserting that he would erase her middle name from the memories of the people who'd given it to her so that no one could bind her. No one except him. *He was only trying to protect me.*

Ania's words: *"He's a controlling tyrant, who thinks he should make all the rules about how other people use magic."*

Jessica took a deep breath. "But maybe Azrael is right. Maybe I shouldn't have children. Maybe I'll get over it."

"Maybe you won't."

Jessica gave an exasperated hiss. "I thought you wanted me to stay."

Tod's brown eyes looked sad. "I do. I'm trying not to get excited about the idea of you staying. Because no one ever stays."

Jessica leaned forward and brought her mouth to his.

"I'd make babies with you in a heartbeat," he said between kisses, "but that wouldn't solve your p-problem if—" She pulled on the sexual energy radiating off him. Tod groaned. He finished his sentence in a rush. "If Azrael objects to demons in general. Oh, gods, Jessica! Have you gotten better at that, or have I just missed you?"

She snickered. She *had* gotten better at feeding slowly—at keeping the thread of energy just taut enough to enhance pleasure, but not enough to leave her partners weak afterward. Jessica slid a leg over Tod's lap, still kissing. His hands came up to her thighs, sliding back and forth, then around to her ass. "Did you really not watch us swimming?" asked Jessica.

He was breathing deeply. "No, I didn't."

Gods, I believe you. "Too nice," said Jessica against his mouth. "You're too sweet; it's ridiculous."

He responded with a hint of sarcasm. "Not everyone can be Mal."

"Thank the gods," said Jessica.

Tod laughed so hard he stopped kissing. They looked at each other, their faces inches apart, pink-cheeked, the sea breeze ruffling their hair. "Undress me," murmured Jessica, and felt his cock go hard against her thigh. But his fingers did not tear at her clothes. He unfastened her trousers with only the hint of a tremble and slid one hand inside, still over her panties, warm against her sex.

It was Jessica's turn to groan. "More than that."

Tod took his hand away and started unbuttoning her shirt. He got it completely open and bent his mouth to a nipple.

"Oh!" Jessica leaned into him. "Oh, that's good. You sweet, sweet, overly-polite werewolf. Oh!" He nipped her. Before she could decide whether to punish this, he wrapped both arms around her hips and pulled her in tight against his body—her soft breasts pressed to the firm muscles of his chest, her sensitive nipples hard against his warm skin, rubbing over the curly red hair. Jessica tipped her head back, sighing with pleasure as he kissed her throat and shoulders. Her hands wandered up and down the sliding muscles of his sides and back. She pushed his shirt down and he flung it the rest of the way off. Then he did the same with hers.

Tod's hands ran warm over her breasts and back, rubbing and caressing, sliding under the band of her trousers. When they were both so frustrated they could hardly stand it, Jessica backed up so that they could shimmy out of the rest of their clothes. Tod managed this a bit faster, probably because his clothes were simpler.

"Let me help with that." He peeled Jessica's panties off her, and then nudged her down onto her back in the grass. His fingers slid between her legs—the sensation startlingly intimate. "May I kiss you here?" he murmured.

"Oh, yes! Gods, yes!"

Tod pushed her legs apart. He kissed her knee, her inner thigh, the place where her leg met her body. Jessica wanted to wrap her legs around his head and pull him in. She wanted him to lick her, fuck her. She wanted to keep pulling on his magic, because it was *so* delicious—something wild, almost feral. She wanted to eat him up.

No, Jessica told herself. *Not that. You don't want that.*

Tod's warm mouth covered her clit, licked into her tight heat, and Jessica bucked up against him. He licked and sucked until she really did wrap her legs around his head. Her back arched and she gave a whimper as pleasure rippled from her groin through her belly and thighs.

Tod raised his head and looked at her, pupils dilated, cheeks flushed, his lips pink and wet. "Come here," murmured Jessica. She pulled a little harder on his magic without quite meaning to, and Tod's eyes blinked shut.

"Jessica, I am so close…"

She gave a breathless laugh. "Sorry."

He straddled her body on hands and knees. Jessica smirked up at him. "I could make you come without even touching you."

"I know," he said in a whisper. He blinked again as though to clear his vision. "Can you…can you…get yourself there again?"

Jessica thought about it. *Mal could.* "Maybe with a little help…" Jessica sat up and pushed him gently over, leaning back on his elbows in the grass. She straddled his hips and rubbed the length of her wet pussy along his erection. Tod's head dropped back and he gave an entirely unpremeditated moan of exquisite agony. The energy between them jumped, and Jessica could feel the tightness building in her crotch again. "Do you want me to fuck you?" she purred. "How bad do you want it?"

"Jessica, please, please," babbled Tod. "I'll do anything, anything, please…"

Jessica rubbed herself up and down his shaft, teasing him, teasing herself, getting closer. "Can I say that you have puppy dog eyes? Because you do, and they're so cute."

Tod raised his head and tried to look indignant. "If you were anyone else, I would tell you to fuck off."

She leaned forward, her voice full of mischief. "Puppy... I just made you sit." She spoke between kisses. "I know I can make you stay. And I bet I can make you..."

She changed her angle and pressed the length of his cock deep inside her. Tod sobbed against her mouth. Jessica tasted the wild sweetness of his magic as the orgasm crashed through him. And she came, too, thighs clenched savagely around his hips, her hands gentle on his face.

6

Azrael

Azrael had planned to spend the afternoon in his tower, working on methods to make sure his own spell-work did not mingle in some disastrous way with that of his guests'. However, he stopped by his apartments to change clothes and to pick up a few things first. When he and Mal came through the door, Lucrecia was sitting at the kitchen table, writing a letter.

She was dressed, as usual, as though she intended to attend a soirée. Her gown was pale blue today, velvet for the cooler temperatures, with her perennial mink half-cape draped across her shoulders. Her silky white hair hung in waves, darkening to pepper at the tips

Mal rolled his eyes when he saw her. "Is she just wandering around now?"

Azrael did not dignify this with a response. He had, in truth, left a clothespin around the bulb of Lucy's perfume bottle, so that she could come and go at will. This arrangement gave her more freedom, but of course she could have also caused a lot of mischief. Azrael trusted Lucy, her long-time rivalry with Mal notwithstanding. The open bottle did leave her vulnerable to magical attack, but Azrael wasn't worried about that in his own rooms. *With the possible exception of Mal, and I don't think he'd risk my hurt and anger.*

Lucy looked up and gave Azrael a toothy grin. For just an instant, her peacock-blue eyes flashed as golden as her dragon scales. "Darling, how was your ride?"

"Invigorating!" said Azrael. He knew he sounded uncharacteristically enthusiastic. He didn't care. "We disposed of two chimeras from the spell traps. It's good to be home."

Lucy's eyes drifted to Mal as though it pained her. "Yes, well, I'm glad to know that the *perimeter* wards, at least, are still in place."

Azrael had to stop himself from flinching. He hadn't told her that Mal could take down his wards. It should not have surprised him that she'd figured it out. Lucy was looking at Azrael as though she knew exactly what he was thinking and was about to express her opinion on this course of action.

Instead, Mal spoke in a malevolent rumble. He was still in panther form, and his teeth flashed white against his night-black fur. "Yes, Lucy, the perimeter wards are unbreached. Nothing is anywhere that it shouldn't be." He did not bother to keep the smirk out of his voice.

"Is that so?" murmured Lucy, matching his combative tone. "Are you planning on doing any magic of your own to entertain the guests? I'm sure they would find that fascinating in the extreme."

Mal came forward and put his front paws on the kitchen table, leaning into her face. "I don't know, but I'm sure I could perform the trick of putting you back in your bottle."

Lucy flickered, as though she were thinking about turning into a dragon. Azrael felt a stab of frustration through the haze of his happiness. *All these years, and they still pick fights with each other.* Mal was, without a doubt, the stronger demon. There was no surprise in this, since he was an astral entity, and Lucy had a mortal parent. Indeed, the odd thing was how evenly they were matched when she was well-rested. Aloud, Azrael said, "Stop antagonizing each other."

Lucy returned her attention to her letter. Mal took his paws off the table. Lucy spoke to Azrael without looking up, "His aura is shot through with your magic, and he can't cloak worth a damn. The High Council will find that alarming. You might want to stop making it worse, at least until they leave."

Azrael shut his eyes and massaged the bridge of his nose. *Of course. I wonder how many other ways I'm embarrassing myself without realizing it.* "Noted."

Lucy continued in the same neutral tone without looking up from her page. "Can Jacob come with Loudain and Lady S?"

Mal reacted first. "You want to invite a demon hunter onto the Shrouded Isle?!"

Lucy ignored Mal, raising her eyes to Azrael. He hesitated.

Mal paced around the room. "A demon hunter who knows my name? Have you lost your mind? Wait a moment… That's who you've been writing letters to, isn't it? Hell's teeth, are you still seeing him? Is he your boyfriend? This is not alright!"

Azrael ignored Mal's histrionics and looked at Lucy. "Jacob was already coming with the main group. You want him to come early?"

Mal's voice rose an octave. "He was already *coming?!*"

Lucy nodded, still looking at Azrael.

Azrael considered. Jacob was a powerful sorcerer, perhaps with as much innate skill as Azrael himself, but Jacob was far older. He had strong views about astral demons, whom he believed were abused by sorcerers and should be returned to the astral plane for their own good and everybody else's. He'd made an exception for Mal, at least partially because of Lucy's influence. Jacob didn't trust Mal, though, and Azrael didn't trust Jacob. He'd been surprised when Lucy kept writing to the man. He'd been even more surprised when she started receiving letters in return. Azrael had forced himself not to read them. "You trust him?"

"I do," said Lucy, her voice still neutral. Her aura showed no emotions. Lucy had always been excellent at cloaking.

"Alright," said Azrael at last. "I'll invite him. Or you can. Does he know Loudain and Lady S?"

"He does." Lucy returned her attention to the page. Azrael almost wished Mal wasn't here so that they could have a real conversation about this. *Later.*

Mal had stopped pacing. He came forward and tried to read over Lucy's shoulder. She promptly turned the sheet over and folded her slender, be-ringed fingers above it with a long-suffering expression. "You can't hide desire from me," growled Mal. "I'm an incubus."

"You can't just take what you like from me," countered Lucy. "I'm a dragon. Besides," she continued with acid sweetness, "who used seduction to keep your fluffy tail on the mortal plane three weeks ago? That would be me. Maybe Azrael is right about you becoming more human. You're so human, you've lost your touch."

"Oh for fuck's sake," muttered Azrael as he sifted through the books on the table.

Of course Mal took the bait. "Stop cloaking for a moment, and we'll all see if I'm losing my touch!"

"Can't. No time to squabble with you right now. I have letters to write."

Mal's voice became plaintive. "Lucy, he's a demon hunter!"

Lucy looked up sharply. "Shh! Listen."

Mal's ears flicked. After an instant, he said, "I don't hear anything."

Lucy leaned in close. "That's the sound of me not asking you for relationship advice."

Mal rolled his eyes. "Fuck off."

Lucy shrugged and flipped the sheet of paper back over. "I told you I have terrible taste in men."

Mal sounded baffled. "Then why don't you like me?"

Lucy laughed—really laughed, her thin shoulders shaking. Azrael smiled into his pile of books. Mal heaved a sigh. "Is that why you and Ren get along so well? Because you both have terrible taste in—?"

Azrael decided this had gone on long enough. "Mal, come tell me what you think of this."

He shuffled one of the new books out of the stack and laid it on the table in front of Mal. The volume was bound in what felt like calfskin dyed a deep, velvety blue. The cover was embossed in gold and silver—a night sky with a bright moon and stars. The letters of the title looped and curled in graceful calligraphy: Book of Dreams.

Mal examined it—first a mundane inspection, then, Azrael could tell, magically. He turned into a man, picked the book up, and turned it over. The back cover had no words, merely an elaborate ouroboros in silver and gold—a serpent eating its tail, the symbol of eternity. Mal's gem-green eyes narrowed as he scanned for auras or energy signatures. Azrael already knew he wouldn't find anything. Finally, Mal turned his attention to Azrael's face, puzzled. "Is it a story? Is this our new bedtime reading?"

For answer, Azrael opened the book, and Mal looked down at it. "Ah…" he began. "I see. It's…" He looked up and stopped. Azrael smiled.

Mal's expression grew puzzled. He looked down at the book again, then back up. He looked down, licked his lips and concentrated fiercely. "Well, it's obviously…um… It's all about…" His voice trailed off as he grew lost in whatever he was reading.

Azrael shut the book and Mal made a noise of protest. "Hey! I was just about to…to…Well, bugger all! What's wrong with it? An encryption charm?"

"Something like that," said Azrael. "You can read it for as long as you like, and you think you're following along, but you can't articulate what you're reading, and as soon as you look away, you forget the whole thing. It's memory magic—something simple, but elegant. I'd like to figure out how it was done." Azrael was, himself, an expert on memory magic. He also prided himself in breaking encryption charms placed upon books.

Lucy had raised her head and was studying the book across the table. "It's got a very faint aura."

"Really?" Azrael frowned, pulling on Mal's magic to take another look. "I don't see one."

Lucy cocked her head. "Hmm. Very faint. Maybe I'm imagining it. Anyway, that looks like a dreamcatcher."

"That's what I thought, too," said Azrael. "My agent bought it at auction in Istor from another collector. Its origins are unclear. I'm assuming the previous owner did not want their dreams read, so they encrypted it. A kind of journal. Anyway, I thought I'd take a crack at it in my tower…in between preparations for our guests. After a shower and change of clothes, of course. I think I've still got chimera juice on this shirt."

7

Mal

Mal followed Azrael out through the hidden staircase that led from his apartments down into his library. The enormous, airy room seemed exceptionally cheerful today. The domed ceiling did not have skylights, but Azrael had put a spell on it recently that mimicked that effect, sending streams of diffuse sunlight between the tall bookcases.

Even the projections from the pocket worlds seemed well-behaved and peaceful. Azrael and Mal passed a young woman with an enormous sword, talking to a centaur girl. *They're not even from the same book,* thought Mal. *They can't get into each other's books now, can they?* Birds were singing in the dome today. Mal was pretty sure they were also projections, but their liquid song made the library feel even more like the forest Mal always imagined—*his* forest, with bookcase trees and a thousand doorways to a thousand worlds, the proper home for a magical panther.

Azrael was humming under his breath, obviously lost in thought as he made his way through the meandering stacks towards his tower. Magicians liked towers because they could be insulated with a complete envelope of wards. Warded structures on the ground were trickier, because the earth beneath them had a constantly changing magical signature, especially this close to the Shattered Sea. Azrael's tower, on the other hand, had multiple concentric bubbles of wards that concentrated his own power, kept him safe from outside interference, and protected his servants and guests from anything he might accidentally unleash. He could work more quickly in the tower, and he could manage spells he would never have attempted elsewhere. It was essentially his laboratory.

Mal was rarely invited into the tower. Azrael could draw magic from Mal's collar at quite a distance when they were on the Shrouded Isle. He did not need Mal in the tower in order to use him, and Azrael was vulnerable when he was working major spells. He usually ordered Mal to wait by the arched entrance to the stairs. Mal stretched out there today. He wondered whether any of the people from the books would come talk to him. He wondered whether Jessica might.

Azrael hesitated beneath the arch. "You know you don't have to stay down here."

Mal looked up in surprise. "I always stay down here." He could almost hear Jessica saying, *"Cats hate change."* *But I don't!* thought Mal. *I just...* "Really?"

Azrael made a come-along motion with his hand and started briskly up the steps. Those steps were one of the reasons

Mal would never have a pudgy master. After an instant's hesitation, Mal bounded up after him.

"It's not a race!" snapped Azrael as the panther whipped around him.

"You love to race!" shot Mal.

"Only when I'm on a horse!"

"Yes, I wonder why?"

Mal was waiting smugly by the heavy, iron-banded door when Azrael arrived—not winded, because he did this all the time, but still breathing deeply, because it was a *lot* of stairs. Mal had carried him down those stairs not long ago with Jessica's hand on Mal's shoulder to keep him human. Mal had been weak and drained of magic after healing Azrael from an all but fatal injury. He'd carried him flung over his shoulder like a sack of potatoes.

I could have held you. Unconscious. That's the only way you would have let me back then. Why didn't I?

Because admitting I wanted to was like opening a wound, he answered himself. *I had to keep focusing on all the reasons I was angry with you. They were good reasons, so that wasn't hard.*

Mal glanced up at Azrael sidelong as he unlocked the door. *You're really going to let me in here.* Azrael didn't look conflicted about it. His pale skin was flushed with the climb, the horseback ride, the hot shower. He looked relaxed and focused on the problem in front of him. He did not look like a man about to let his summoned incubus into his private sanctuary. Then again, Azrael had his wards back in place, and Mal could see nothing beyond them.

The inside of the tower was much as Mal remembered from his handful of visits: high, narrow windows, a large desk dominating one wall, an intimidating black sword hanging above the desk. Cabinets and work tables stood around the edges of the room, covered in books, candles, and materials for spells. There were several enormous bags of salt, iron filings, and silver scrap. The center of the room was completely bare except for a carefully chalked circle. It was etched in runes, reinforced with faint lines of old blood and salt and iron. A summoning circle.

Azrael walked straight through it on the way to his desk, but Mal skirted it out of habit. Azrael took the Book of Dreams out of his bag and laid it on the desk. He muttered over it for a few moments—spells of binding and revealing, preparation work. He leaned across the desk to fish a vial out of a drawer, then poured out a dab of oil and drew a circle around the book on the smooth wood.

Mal sat at his side, listening with half an ear, still looking around the room. He was remembering the handful of occasions over the years when Azrael had needed him here.

Azrael broke off to say, "You don't have to be a panther, either, if you don't want to."

Mal almost said, "But I'm always a panther in here." *Why do I say that so often?* He shot up into a man and leaned against the desk, enjoying the fact that he was now half a head taller than Azrael. He'd given himself a comfortable shirt and trousers—the sort of clothing he could easily make with magic. He didn't bother with shoes. Mal looked at his own hands in wonder. "I was never allowed to have thumbs in here."

"Thumbs can get you into trouble," agreed Azrael. He'd selected a bone pen from a jar on his desk (a jar made from the skull of a carnivorous toad-owl, Mal noted) and begun to trace flowing lines of magic into the cover of the book. The volume glowed faintly in response—not a product of Azrael's work, but a sign of resistance from the encryption spell.

Mal glanced up at the huge, black sword. "You threatened to cut my head off with that once."

Azrael stumbled over his work. His eyes skittered up and back down again. "You asked a courtier to take off your collar. You nearly killed her."

Mal nodded. "You made her forget."

"Yes, I am the only person who remembers the extremely unpleasant thing you did to her face."

"Sorry."

Azrael said nothing.

Mal's eyes flitted around the room. "When you made all those one-way jumps for dealing with the vampires in Solaria, you kept me up here. You made me sit in the doorway."

"I needed your input," agreed Azrael. "I remember you had plenty to say."

"*I* remember I wanted to bend you over your desk," muttered Mal.

Azrael's hands kept moving over the book. He didn't react at all. But Mal *felt* the tug on his magic falter.

That's interesting. Mal leaned against the desk and gave a piratical grin. "I'm sure I said so at the time."

"I'm sure I told you to stop talking at the time," said Azrael, his eyes focused on the dreamcatcher. It had begun to emit a faint odor like green wood burning.

"You did," said Mal. "And I did. Because I had to. But you can't actually shut me up with a word anymore."

"Can't I?" snapped Azrael.

"Bend you over your desk on top of all those stupid books," murmured Mal, "and make you forget everything you ever read. Show you some real memory magic. That's what I said at the time."

Azrael's face was completely closed. Not the faintest flicker of emotion or desire escaped through his wards. And yet, again, Mal felt that curious stutter in the flow of magic between them. *Why didn't I notice before?*

Because he would have already shut me up before, Mal answered himself.

They were standing very close, side by side. All Mal had to do was turn, and he was standing behind Azrael. He didn't touch him, though. He just stood close enough to smell his soap, and put his fingertips on the desk on either side. Mal brought his mouth a whisker's breadth from Azrael's right ear and murmured, "Did you want me to? Back then?"

Azrael's control of Mal's magic jangled like a discordant harp string. Mal felt a rush of smug satisfaction. It wasn't as good as being able to see his desires, but it was a lot easier than trying to read his face. As if in added confirmation, the ear Mal had just spoken into was turning pink. Azrael's voice came out an octave lower than usual and a little hoarse. "Mal, I am trying to work."

"I know," purred Mal. "You should definitely keep working. You have a lot do."

Azrael stopped and put down the bone pen, spreading his fingers on the desk with a put-upon air. "I asked you up here because I could use your opinion about a containment spell for our visitors and their hangers-on. I never intended to host other magicians on my island. Nothing on my estate is set up for it. The sorcerers may bring demons. Lady S certainly will."

He was talking faster and faster. Mal didn't interrupt, didn't move closer, didn't touch him. "I can't just strip them of magic; they'll regard that as a threat. We need some kind of magical airlock that will allow us to identify dangerous cross-effects and deal with them in a controlled environment. I might need you to simulate outside magic—something very different from mine so we could test it. Do you think you could do that?"

"Yes," drawled Mal, his voice an unhurried counterpoint to Azrael's tumble of words. "But you haven't answered my question." *I backed you up against this desk the last time we were up here and kissed you against your will. I shredded your wards, and that was the closest I've ever come to assaulting someone. I won't do that again.*

Azrael retrieved his pen with a noise of exasperation. The book under his hands was still glowing faintly, still emitting an odor. He opened it and began sinking magic directly into the pages. The book began to smoke. "If you are going to do something," he said between gritted teeth, "do it. Otherwise, stop breathing down my neck."

Mal considered this. "No." He relished the word. He'd so rarely gotten to use it. "Answer the question."

Azrael swallowed. "Yes." He spoke like a man admitting to murder. "Happy?"

"Oh, I've been happy for weeks." Mal put his hands on Azrael's hips, eliciting a gratifying intake of a breath. He continued in an unhurried purr. "Do you still want me to?"

"Mal, *look* at where we are."

"I know. It's dreadfully transgressive." Mal's right hand drifted from Azrael's hip and slid between two buttons of his shirt. Of course Azrael was wearing an undershirt, but at least it was thin. Mal traced his naval through the warm fabric. "Take your time. Think about it. And then tell me." He spoke now with his lips pressed against Azrael's burning ear.

"Mal," Azrael had given up all efforts to control his voice, "I am in the middle of this. If I stop now, the enchantment will destroy the book."

"I know." Mal kissed his ear, ran his tongue around the rim. The thread of magic between them wobbled and jerked in a way that Mal found intoxicating. But he could see that Azrael was starting to sweat.

"It's not like you're doing something very important," said Mal in a normal voice. "It's just a dreamcatcher. Only I'm sort of enjoying the challenge. How is this different from racing?"

He felt the tension in Azrael's neck ease. *You need to be reminded you can step outside the game. You forget if I don't tell you.*

Azrael swallowed. "Alright. Challenge accepted. Just don't take down my wards here."

"I won't. But if you will not let me see what you need, you are going to have to answer questions."

Azrael grunted and returned the whole of his attention to the book. The flow of magic between them steadied. Mal buried his face against the side of Azrael's neck and brought one hand up over his thumping heart. The man smelled of soap and very faintly of horse. His hair was damp. Mal hadn't thought, at first, that he liked Azrael's hair short. Azrael had worn it shoulder-length most of his life—fine and straight and ink black. He'd cut it close after Mal left. That's how he'd turned up in the Provinces when he'd come looking for them. *"Cats hate change,"* Mal heard Jessica say again in his head.

Bollocks. There *were* some nice things about short hair— namely that Mal could see more of Azrael's sinewy neck and pale throat, pretty as a girl's.

Azrael's heart was hammering under Mal's palm, the blood beating under Mal's tongue, but the tug of magic didn't falter. If anything, Azrael pulled harder. *Now he knows it's a game. And he hates to lose.*

Azrael's chest was rising and falling rapidly, but he didn't make a sound. Mal nuzzled into the sensitive skin under his jaw, kissing and sucking.

Azrael finally made a noise so low it might have been inaudible, except that Mal had his lips against the warm throat. He felt the sound vibrate over his skin. He growled and pulled Azrael tighter against him. Azrael responded by pulling harder on Mal's magic. The book's green-leaf-burning odor strengthened as its encryption spell continued to resist Azrael's assault.

Mal's fingers flipped shirt buttons. He untucked Azrael's undershirt and slid a hand against bare skin. Azrael hissed between his teeth.

"You're being awfully aggressive with that thing," murmured Mal, his fingers trailing delicately over Azrael's chest. "If you don't employ a little more finesse, you'll burn it up before you break it."

Azrael said nothing. He didn't whimper when Mal's thumb brushed across a nipple, although he stopped breathing for a moment. Mal knew that Azrael could shut out the world. His life had been full of situations that required absolute focus for complex tasks while under intense pressure. Azrael could shut out the world. *But he can't shut out me—not completely. Because he's using my magic.*

Mal was sure Azrael could feel his erection pressing against his ass. *You could tell me to get away from you. I would. But you don't actually want me to.*

He looked down at Azrael's hands, at his long, delicate fingers around the bone pen, tracing runes with fierce attention. He was pulling a *lot* of magic from the collar. Mal wondered whether the dreamcatcher really was *that* well-encrypted or whether Azrael was just too distracted to work efficiently.

Mal flipped the clasp on Azrael's belt buckle and slid one hand into his trousers without bothering to unfasten them. Azrael made a noise like a strangled cat.

"That feels almost painful," said Mal cheerfully, rubbing Azrael's cock in the tight space and loving the way the muscles of his legs quivered.

Mal raised his head and caught a reflection of them in the mirrored door of a cabinet: Azrael's flushed face and expression of ferocious concentration, his head tipped a little sideways from Mal's attention, Mal tight against him, one hand inside his shirt, the other down his pants. *We are doing this in your tower,* he thought and shivered. They were surrounded by implements used to trap and kill magical beings, spells of dangerous power, a place where the world had been made thin by too much passage…and a summoning circle a few steps away.

"Don't take down my wards here."

I won't, Mal reminded himself. *But I am going to win this race if you don't finish what you're doing in less than two minutes.* Azrael's cock was leaking fluid against his fingers. Mal worked him harder, feeling the muscles of his belly and thighs tighten, his breath coming in rasps.

There was an audible pop and an explosion of sparks. For one moment, Mal thought the book really had caught fire. It was still intact when the smoke cleared, however. Azrael slammed it shut and shoved it away. "Done! It's done! Dear gods. Fuck. That was one of the toughest encryption charms I've ever seen. Fuck!"

"And yet you broke it in record time!" said Mal, still stroking Azrael's cock, the thumb of his other hand flicking back and forth across a nipple. "See how helpful I am?"

Azrael groaned and leaned into him. He pressed his ass hard against Mal's erection. "Ask for it," said Mal, his voice thick.

"Please." Azrael tilted his head up and sideways towards Mal's face, black eyes desperate. Mal's hand slid to Azrael's throat, pushing his shirt up as he went—encircling the slender neck possessively, almost threateningly. He felt Azrael's second "please" vibrate through his fingers.

Mal kissed him on the mouth. With the hand that wasn't around his throat, Mal unfastened Azrael's trousers. They fell with a clatter of belt buckle. Azrael flinched at the noise, but Mal didn't give him time to think about it. He pushed him down onto his desk and pulled off his underwear in the same movement. Everything landed around his ankles and Mal kicked the clothes away. *Real clothes are terribly inconvenient.* Mal made his own disappear, melting back into his essence.

He leaned forward, his cock pressing against the crease of Azrael's ass, relishing the sight of his master facedown in what looked like a grimoire, a couple of ledgers, and a scattering of pens that had fallen from the overturned toad-owl skull. Azrael was scrabbling to push things out of the way, but Mal brought a forearm down across his shoulders and ended that nonsense. *Who has sex across a desk and tries to make sure it's tidy while he's doing it?*

My ridiculous master, that's who. Looks like you need more distraction.

Mal leaned close to Azrael's ear, letting the weight of his body plaster the smaller man against the desk until Azrael could barely breathe. He kept his forearm across Azrael's shoulders like an iron bar, pinning him in place, pressing his cheek against the ancient leather of a grimoire that looked like it probably contained numerous methods of binding demons.

Mal wondered if a book had ever been written by a demon on how to bend a sorcerer over his desk in his own tower and fuck him until he couldn't see straight.

Astral incubi only fuck their summoners once.

Mal shook his head to clear it. They were both breathing hard. He stroked Azrael's flank with his free hand, gliding it all the way up his taut body to his face. He stroked his cheek, his lips, forced two fingers past his teeth into his warm mouth. Azrael's breath came in shallow, panting rasps around Mal's fingers, his tongue an uncoordinated muscular wetness, moving over Mal's fingertips. His eyes were screwed shut, his hands in fists on either side of his head.

Mal leaned close to his ear. "We can't do this without something slick."

Azrael's eyes snapped open. He tried to speak around Mal's fingers, but Mal just pushed them deeper into his mouth. "Go on. Make the spell. I know you can."

Azrael's eyes flicked up at him, huge and frustrated. He was still trying to talk. Mal licked the back of Azrael's neck as though he'd been the panther. "Come on, world's-most-powerful-sorcerer. Can't make something slippery in your own tower without your hands?" Mal rubbed his cock back and forth along the crease of Azrael's ass, feeling his legs tremble.

Mal could feel him *trying* to focus, trying to find a way to make the spell work without hands or voice, trying to use Mal's magic through the haze of his desire. The sensation was shockingly arousing. Mal groaned against his neck. "That tickles in all the best ways. You'd better hurry up or I'm just going to finish and you can get yourself off."

Azrael made a noise of protest and bucked up against him. "What was that? Go ahead and fuck me without oil? No. I don't want to hurt you *that* much."

Oh, but I do, whispered a voice in Mal's head. He ignored it.

He withdrew his fingers just enough for Azrael to jerk his own head back. "You malevolent bastard," he spat. "I am *trying!*"

"Try harder."

Before Mal could curl his fingers into his mouth again, Azrael reeled off the spell, the runes shimmering visibly in the air for a moment. Because he'd used only his mouth and not his hands, the slippery liquid came spilling out between his lips to land in Mal's cupped palm. Azrael coughed and sputtered. He started swearing again, but before he could get too worked up about it, Mal pressed a slicked finger into his ass. That shut him up.

Azrael was tight with nerves. Mal wished he could use his own magic. A little feeding, and Azrael would have become calm and pliant. He would have been relaxed and unafraid.

And unsafe, Mal reminded himself. *What might come through that summoning circle in response to an unwarded sorcerer so close on the other side? Forget the circle. What might be waiting in this very room to pounce? No, no, leave his wards alone.*

"Just do it," Azrael hissed. "Mal, just fuck me; I don't care if it hurts."

Mal drew back to put both hands on Azrael's hips, letting him breathe. He pressed the head of his cock against the slick ring of muscle. He started to push forward, but then Azrael pressed back, catching him by surprise, enveloping Mal's dick in tight heat.

Azrael was breathing in ragged gasps. Mal didn't thrust for a moment. He leaned over Azrael again, kissing the back of his neck. "Mine," he murmured. *My summoner, my sorcerer, my human, mine, mine, mine.*

Azrael gave another impatient shove, and Mal moved—slowly at first, then picking up speed as Azrael's body allowed it. Azrael was squirming and groaning, sobbing for breath. Mal moved back enough to catch one of his legs under the knee and drag it up onto the desk, spreading him wider, splaying his body flat across his books and papers and vials and pens. Mal brought down his weight across Azrael's back and shoulders, thrusting so hard that he lifted Azrael's remaining foot off the ground. *You want to feel helpless? How's that?*

Snap!

A dizzy wave of desire crashed over Mal's demon senses—fear mixed with arousal, dark longing, a need to be obliterated.

For an instant, Mal panicked. *I took down your wards! How? I wasn't trying.*

And then he realized he hadn't. Azrael had done it himself. *Fuck.*

And then Mal was feeding, because he could not help it, because Azrael was radiating sexual energy, and it was—*he* was—the most delicious thing Mal had ever tasted. Feeding on him felt as natural as breathing. It felt like a dislocated joint coming back into place, a missing puzzle piece, a musical note that had been off-key sliding into true.

Stop, thought Mal distantly. *This is too much. You're taking too much.*

There is no such thing as too much, whispered the voice of Lust. *This is what you were created to do. He fed on you for twenty years, and now it is your turn. This is exactly where you've always wanted him.*

Azrael's movements were growing weaker, less coordinated. Mal knew that his feeding was creating a narcotic rush of pleasure that Azrael was in no frame of mind to resist. *He's not going to tell me to stop.*

I am Lust. I am insatiable.

Jessica's voice: *"You are yourself."*

Mal's eyes snapped open. *I am myself. A being bound in time to other people by choice. And I have a tomorrow.* We *have a tomorrow. But only if I stop.*

It took every ounce of his self-control to clamp down on the dwindling flow of magic. Azrael's pulse was beating erratically against Mal's skin. Mal had certainly taken too much.

Wallace's words from what seemed like a lifetime ago: *"Does he give you his magic in the ass?"*

Worth a try, thought Mal, and poured the magic back into the sorcerer beneath him.

Azrael came so hard, his hips curled off the desk for a moment. The intensity of his pleasure tipped Mal over the edge, and he emptied himself inside Azrael's shuddering body.

Mal lay there on top of him for a moment, their rasping breath barely audible over the blood beating in his ears. At last, he managed, "Ren?"

Azrael made a muffled noise. He was lying with his cheek against a crumpled page, all attempts to push himself up on elbows and hands forgotten. Mal released the arm he had looped under one of Azrael's legs. He stood up, then caught Azrael with both hands as he almost slithered to the floor.

Mal dragged him to his feet, and Azrael leaned heavily on the desk. His eyes were still shut. His shirt was unbuttoned, his undershirt pushed halfway to his neck. He was naked from the waist down except for his shoes.

Mal's entire being was diffuse with sorcerous magic. He felt electric, as though he were made of light. Indeed, he was surprised not to find himself physically glowing. After a moment's consideration, he crouched enough to get his arm under both of Azrael's knees and scooped him off his feet.

That elicited a gasp of surprise. Azrael's arms clenched instinctively around Mal's neck to keep from falling. He spoke in a guttural rasp, "What are you doing?"

"Holding you," said Mal cheerfully. *The way I wish I had last time I carried you out of here.* Mal was broader, but not that much taller, and Azrael's long legs dangled over his arm as he came around the desk and flopped down in the big chair behind it. He pulled Azrael's head up against his neck, arranged his legs over the arm of the chair, and leaned back, petting Azrael's short hair, enjoying the way it felt almost like fur.

Azrael didn't struggle, didn't say anything else. He relaxed. Mal's emotions ricocheted between profound contentment and creeping guilt. At last, he said, "That was dangerous. We shouldn't have done it."

Azrael gave a grunt that could have meant anything.

Mal stroked his hair. "You should tell me not to do it again."

Another grunt.

"Boss."

"I'm not your boss."

"You are *mine,* though." He hadn't meant to say that out loud.

"Obviously," muttered Azrael. "Unfortunately. Terrifyingly." He hesitated. "Utterly."

Something curled in Mal's belly—not arousal, but something adjacent and more fragile. He didn't know how to respond, so he kept stroking Azrael's hair and face. After a moment, Azrael cleared his throat and said, "Are you healing me with magic? I keep thinking I should be sore...as much as we've been doing this. I wondered if I should have trouble sitting a horse this morning. Then I realized I don't actually know. I have no idea what's normal."

Mal snickered. "There are a few advantages to bedding an incubus."

"So the answer is yes?"

Mal shrugged. "I suppose you'll find out when you let some mortal fuck you morning, noon, and night."

"In that case, I will resign myself to mysteries."

"Can we reenact this for Jessica? She would enjoy it tremendously."

"Well, I'm not sure she'd fit in this chair," said Azrael critically, "but we can…" He ran a hand across his face. "Gods."

"We should definitely reenact it," said Mal, "except for the part where you took down your wards and I almost ate you." He tipped Azrael's face up. He scanned the dark eyes, so full of… something. "That scared me," Mal whispered. He didn't think Azrael looked sufficiently worried, so he repeated, "I almost ate you."

"But you didn't," Azrael whispered back.

Mal's face crumpled. "Boss…"

"I'm not—"

"Sometimes I need you to be!"

Azrael's expression changed, and he put a hand on Mal's neck, long fingers threading up into his hair. "Alright. Shhh. I didn't know it would scare you." After a moment, he said, "Shall I give you the shopping list of things I want you to do today? Is that bossy enough?"

Mal laughed. He wished he didn't feel so twitchy. He shifted his weight, reached out to steady himself on the desk, and a drawer popped open under his fingers. Mal stared at it in surprise.

Azrael turned to look. "Ah."

Mal stared at his hand, then back at the drawer. "Why did it do that?"

"It thinks you're me."

Mal gaped. "But—"

"It's keyed to my magical signature. Most of the cabinets are, as well. Half the locked doors in the palace—"

Mal clapped a hand over Azrael's mouth. "Why are you telling me that? Stop telling me that!"

Azrael jerked his head away. "You just had me over my desk in my tower without a scrap of wards between us. You think I'm worried about my cabinets?"

Mal felt a rush of irrational panic. "We can't do this again. I don't want to do this again!"

Azrael leaned his head against Mal's chest. "You don't want me on my knees in a summoning circle?" He said it so softly, almost without inflection, as though he were discussing the guest menu. And yet all of Mal's senses twanged at once.

Azrael buried his face against Mal's chest and laughed.

"You are teasing me!" said Mal with a confused mixture of disbelief, indignation, and delight.

Azrael turned, his movements increasingly brisk and coordinated, reaching for the Book of Dreams. He pulled it into his lap, opened it, and made a sound of disgust. "I was afraid of that. I should have been more careful."

Mal looked down and saw that the pages were blank. The words he'd read a couple of hours ago—so interesting, but so impossible to remember—had vanished. "It was probably charmed to erase itself when you broke the seal," said Mal. "It would have done that no matter how you broke it."

Azrael nodded. "A little more finesse might have gotten around the trigger, though. Too much brute force." He yawned.

"You were distracted," said Mal. He started buttoning Azrael's shirt.

Azrael scrubbed his hands over his face. "I have done something unspeakable to my desk. Gods. Do you ever wonder five minutes after sex why you thought that was a good idea?"

"No," said Mal loftily. "I'm an incubus. It's always a good idea. Except for the part where I nearly ate you and you sort of wanted me to." He shouldn't have added that last bit. It was the part that scared him most, and he shouldn't have said it. Mal tensed.

Azrael didn't say anything. He stood up from Mal's lap and walked around the desk. He put on his trousers, put his wards back together, and set to work cleaning up the "unspeakable" mess. Mal joined him, creating some clothes for himself as he did. They were putting the last of the pens back into the toad-owl when Azrael said, "I don't want you to kill me."

"But it felt like that," said Mal. "It's my nature to want to eat you…to kill you, Ren, and it's also my nature to fulfill your desires. If you point those two things in the same direction…"

Azrael took a deep breath and looked at the ceiling. "There are times when I feel trapped in my own head. You take me right out of it. That's what I want. That's…what you're sensing, I think. I don't want to leave. Not permanently. I love what we're making here."

Mal uncoiled a little. "Talk to me more. When we're fucking."

"Alright."

"And gods, I do want you on your knees in a summoning circle!"

Azrael smiled down at his desk. He positively grinned. Mal didn't think he'd ever seen him smile like that.

"We could…" began Mal, but Azrael waved his hand. "Magical airlock! Guests! Wards! Testing!"

"But—"

"No buts. That is what we are doing right now." Azrael opened a cabinet and began hunting for materials.

He's in such a good mood. I should mention the other thing. Mal took a deep breath and spoke to his back. "Boss…you like demons."

Azrael paused to glance over his shoulder. "A bizarre observation, all things considered."

Mal shuffled his feet. "I mean, we're your best friends."

Azrael continued digging through the cabinet and said nothing.

"It's just… Jessica…"

Azrael emerged with an ornate bottle in one hand and an onyx pangolin idol in the other. "These will do for test anchors. I will need you to simulate some alien magic. Can you do that with your aura full of mine? Oh, hells, probably not. Here, I bet we can use something from the spell traps."

Mal sighed. He should have brought this up when Azrael was still feeling cuddly. He went from cuddly to prickly in the blink of an eye. "Jessica…"

Mal couldn't tell whether Azrael knew what Mal wanted to say and didn't want to hear it or whether he was completely focused on his airlock. "Jessica, what? Spit it out, Mal."

Mal gave up. "We wish you'd come to the Revels with us," he finished lamely.

Azrael turned way. "No. Here, hold this pangolin for a moment."

8

Jessica

Jessica got back to Azrael's rooms just as the clock struck six. *My rooms now, too,* she reminded herself. She was hungry, having finished her snacks and picnic meal long ago. She intended to grab a bite—just so that she wouldn't be embarrassingly famished at the Revels—and change clothes before leaving again.

She unlocked the door and came hurrying through the sitting room into the kitchen with such speed that she startled Azrael at some task over the kitchen table. He jumped like a nervous rabbit and brought his hand down over whatever he'd been working on. "Jessica. I thought… Mal left for the party half an hour ago."

"I've been up in the hills," panted Jessica. "Yuli and I found the most amazing sunken bathhouse! I just need to eat something and change." She rooted around in the cabinets and icebox, emerged with cheese and crackers. "I see Mal did not manage to change your mind about attending with us."

"No, I have other things to do." Azrael swept something off the table and dropped it into his pocket. Jessica restrained herself from asking. The explanation would probably be long and technical, and she didn't have time.

She *did* pause to admire a dark blue, beautifully embossed book, featuring a night sky. "I saw that in the new acquisitions earlier," said Jessica. "I can't remember what it's about, though."

"It's a dreamcatcher," said Azrael. "It had an encryption enchantment, which I broke this morning. Rather clumsily, I'm afraid. Whatever dreams had been recorded were erased." He reached out and flipped the book open to demonstrate. The creamy pages were blank.

"Oh. Well, it's pretty anyway. How does it catch dreams?"

"It writes them like a journal," said Azrael. "It might catch a few of ours tonight."

Jessica smiled. She wondered what might flit through her dreams. *Not children, I hope.*

Azrael got up. His respectable charcoal dress pants looked a bit wrinkled, and his white shirt was positively scuffed and stained.

"You and Mal must have worked hard this afternoon."

Azrael said nothing. He moved around her, pulled a mug off a shelf, and poured the tea.

Jessica cocked her head. "Or did he just mess up your clothes?"

Azrael turned and offered her the fragrant mug. "Both. Lord Loudain and Lady S will be arriving in a week, a little ahead of the other guests. I've told Lucy she can invite Jacob. Mal was apoplectic, but that might just be because it was Lucy. Are you comfortable with Jacob coming with the early group?"

Jessica accepted the tea. *That's interesting. I thought Lucy was just setting a hunter off our scent at the Council Meeting.* "Yes. I mean, if Lucy wants him there, who am I to say otherwise?"

Azrael look at her narrowly. "You're a demon. He's a demon hunter."

Jessica shrugged. "We're on your island. I'm your..." *Friend? Playmate? Familiar? Your boyfriend's girlfriend?*

Azrael spoke quickly. "I can certainly protect you here. But...I thought I should ask."

Jessica smiled. "I look forward to meeting him again... under better circumstances."

Azrael nodded. He looked like he wanted to say something else.

Jessica tapped the side of her throat. "You have an....um... Right here."

Azrael shut his eyes and swore.

Jessica sipped her tea. "Just so you know."

He put both hands over his face and rubbed hard. "I'm not used to this. It feels like I'm going to embarrass myself or worse at any moment. And all these strange people showing up on my island in a few days... Mal says, 'Don't let them come.' But I feel like I should."

"I think you should," agreed Jessica. "And it's not easy saying 'no' to Mal...no matter how much simpler it would make your life."

Azrael stared at the ceiling. "I feel like I used up all my 'noes' over the last twenty years. I don't have any 'no' left."

Jessica set down her tea and put her arms around his chest. He encircled her immediately, and she felt him relax a little. Jessica remembered riding behind Azrael on a storybook horse. She'd wrapped her arms around his lean, warm body for balance, but she'd known, then, that she couldn't really hold him. She'd wanted to pull him close, tuck her face against him, feel his body relax to fit her own. But that had seemed as impossible as touching the moon.

And now it wasn't. Now he was right here, talking to her as a person inside his tiny circle of trust. *Will he regard what I want as a betrayal of that trust?*

"You are a good friend," said Azrael against her hair. "I don't know what to do with one lover, let alone two, and he is so much more demanding. But I hope you know, Jessica, how *much* I appreciate you being here."

Jessica rested her cheek against the collar of the shirt Mal had ruined. She inhaled the scent of ink and the bright, green-grass smell of Azrael's magic. Jessica shut her eyes. She *loved* the fact that he trusted her. She didn't want to do or say anything that might make him stop. "Is Lady S the one with the lemur?"

Azrael's voice rumbled pleasantly through his chest and warm clothes. "Yes. He's an aspect of Sloth. She's had him for a long time. I don't know whether he's an astral entity or something earth-born. I don't know whether she's in love with him."

Jessica snickered. "Do people fall in love with other kinds of demons? I mean those who aren't aspects of Lust?"

Azrael shrugged. "No more readily than they fall in love with mortals." He hesitated. "But sorcerers are often a little odd, a little isolated. Demons become our only companions. Long association…"

Jessica nodded. She raised her head and very gently kissed the bruise Mal had left under Azrael's jaw. He made a tiny noise, although she couldn't tell whether it was pleasure or pain. "What did he do?" she whispered. "You don't have to tell me, but you're making me curious."

Azrael gave a jittery laugh. "Turned me over my desk in my tower."

Jessica stifled a snicker against his shirt. "No wonder you've got ink on your clothes." She thought a moment. "It's because he was never allowed up there, you know."

"I know. I said…" Azrael broke off and swallowed. "I have lost my mind."

"I don't think so. Your cock doesn't think so." Jessica could tell that the memory was making him hard.

Azrael laughed again. He sounded like a boy when he did that.

Jessica tilted her head up and kissed him on the mouth—warm and relaxed and a little bristly. His breathing had picked up a bit by the time she pulled away. "I am so tempted to drag you to bed, build a pillow fort, and make you tell me about it in *exquisite* detail."

Azrael cleared his throat. "Mal suggested we…uh…recreate it for you."

Jessica barked a laugh. "However," she continued, "I promised Tod I would dance with him, and he is a particular friend."

Azrael nodded. "I have something to do this evening, as well, something I'm making…for you."

Jessica's eyebrows rose. "How mysterious. My birthday is still months off."

He smiled. "This will be sooner than your birthday."

"Can I have a hint?"

"I fear you must live in suspense."

"Oh!" Jessica stepped away from him with mock disappointment. "Well, then, I will take myself off to the Revels, where the suspense is manageable. See you later this evening."

9

Jessica

The Revels began as Jessica remembered—with masks, music, pretty clothes, drinks, and dancing. Jessica had been to only one such party before, her time and attention having been taken up with Mal and Azrael after that. Unlike other events on the Shrouded Isle, these parties were hosted exclusively for the courtiers and a few of the island's permanent residents. They were not for the entertainment of political guests.

The courtiers enjoyed the Revels as an opportunity to spend time with each other. Occasionally, they formed lasting attachments. Azrael had received more than one wedding invitation from courtiers who'd met here.

However, the more practical purpose was to fully charge Mal's magical energy. Mal did need something to work with, of course. Even he could not create desire where none existed. He could enhance it, though—lower inhibitions, remove guilt, shame, anxiety, and fear.

The courtiers were chosen specifically for their high sexual energy, beauty, and good natures. They were tested before they arrived. Most of them were in their twenties. It wasn't generally difficult to stir things up.

I could do it...in theory, thought Jessica. But she'd only ever tried that with Mal. Whereas he was a demon with a sliver of humanity, Jessica was human with a sliver of demonic nature. Jessica worked best one-on-one.

She'd worn red this evening, like last time—satin, strapless, with a full skirt and black lace around the hem. It wasn't quite Shattered Sea—a little closer to the modern fashions farther inland, a little daring. Azrael had presented her with some adorable black boots a week ago, and the dress allowed them to show just enough. Her mask was white porcelain with red feathers and a black lacy pattern around the eyes. Like all the masks, it only covered the top half of her face. One was likely to need one's mouth for eating, drinking, and other activities.

Jessica hadn't arrived with any of her friends, and she didn't try to find them straight away. The big, fresco-painted ballroom easily swallowed a few hundred courtiers. They danced in the center near the orchestral dais or visited around the edges, where couches and tables with food, drinks, and games were set up. The room opened onto the gardens, full of flaming torches. Jessica glimpsed the big, heated pool, the hedge maze and gazebos beyond. The garden glowed with just enough light to appear friendly and left just enough shadows to provide privacy.

Jessica danced with three men—two she recognized in spite of their masks. They were casual acquaintances from her cohort. The other was from a group a couple of years ahead of Jessica. They certainly wanted her, and she fed off their desires—taking a little energy from each, knowing she'd have ample opportunities before the night was over. Her magic was not low in any case, not after Tod.

She'd been at the party for an hour before she spotted him, sipping a drink and talking to a few of the older staff members behind the orchestra. He was wearing the peacock-blue coat she remembered from last time, complete with gold sash and the white mask with painted swirls of deep blue and purple. He looked so utterly different from his usual servant's livery that only his red hair and Jessica's memories gave him away.

His eyes lit up behind the mask when he saw her. "Excuse me," he told his friends. "I was promised a dance."

Jessica grinned as he took her in his arms. "This time I promise not to make you weak at the knees," she whispered.

"Too late," he whispered back.

"Are those people some of your friends on the staff?" asked Jessica.

He nodded.

"Will they stay all evening?"

Tod shrugged. "Probably not. But they'll play cards for a while and watch."

"I'd like to join them for a bit if you'll introduce us," said Jessica. "I should meet permanent residents if I'm going to be staying here."

"Making yourself lady of the house?" Tod teased.

Jessica shot him an arch look. "How can I? When Mal is already lady of the house!"

Tod snorted a laugh. He stopped suddenly, looking over Jessica's shoulder. "And speaking of Mal. Oh, for gods' sakes."

Jessica turned and saw him. Mal was wearing his beautiful long-tailed, high waisted black coat with silver buttons, but he'd gotten himself a new mask. It was a cat face—black velvet with green swirls around the eyes. The cheeks had been lined with a spray of fine, black feathers that looked like fur. He was talking to several other courtiers, all of whom looked thoroughly fascinated.

Tod and Jessica kept dancing. "Good, he's talking to people," said Jessica. "He needs more friends."

Tod looked incredulous. "Everyone on the Shrouded Isle is his friend!"

"I mean friends he doesn't fuck."

"Good luck with that."

When the song ended, Jessica led Tod somewhat unwillingly to the drink table where Mal was now temporarily alone. He was clearly assessing the energy in the room, deciding what to do with it, humming to himself.

His green eyes glittered behind his mask at Jessica and Tod. "Red and the Wolf. Adorable. But watch out. In this version of the fairytale, *she* eats *you*."

Tod rolled his eyes. "You're a fine one to talk about adorable." He tapped his mask.

Mal grinned even wider. "Shall I get you one with pointy ears? Maybe a fluffy tail?"

Tod picked up a drink. "Fuck off, Mal."

Jessica watched them carefully. She'd never seen Tod and Mal exchange more than a few words, although she knew they'd had a liaison several years ago that had left Tod feeling confused and a little hurt. He was not normally interested in men, and he hadn't known, then, that Mal was an incubus.

Tod clearly found Mal's cheerfully overbearing nature and boundless confidence somewhat grating, especially when it involved getting him into bed. Tod also didn't trust Mal as an astral demon. On a deeper level, Jessica suspected that Tod was a little jealous of Mal's uncomplicated relationship with his shapeshifting. Tod would never be so easy with his own animal nature.

"Have either one of you seen Yuli?" asked Jessica suddenly. "I thought she'd be here."

Mal shook his head.

"Nope," said Tod. "But if she's changed her mask recently, I might not recognize her."

"She's more into watching than fucking," put in Mal unhelpfully.

"Yuli has a boyfriend at home," said Jessica. "She's fond of him. But they both knew what she was getting into when she volunteered as tribute, and she enjoys the parties."

"I know," said Mal with that smug, I-know-everyone's-bedroom-business expression.

Tod spoke without looking up from his glass. "Are we playing outdoor games tonight?"

"I was thinking maybe," said Mal. "It's cool enough."

"Outdoor games?" asked Jessica.

"Yes, in the fall and winter, people need to get their blood moving," said Mal. "It's a little chilly to be taking clothes off otherwise. Sometimes we play games outside. Games where people chase each other are best. I can really get them going when they chase each other."

"Sometimes Capture the Flag," said Tod with a twinkle.

Mal laughed. To Jessica, he said, "He beat me once and has never forgotten."

Tod shrugged. "I take what I can get."

Jessica looked down at her dress. "Capture the Flag…in *these* clothes?"

"I've often thought it was a little unfair to the ladies," said Tod. "Although if you're playing tag at a Midnight Revel, the point really isn't *not* getting caught."

"Not for most people," said Mal to Tod. "Normal people."

"Fuck you," said Tod, this time with more pleasure.

Jessica shook her head. "I am not playing tag in this dress, and it's too cool to play in my underwear."

"You'll just have to find a man who wants to trade clothes with you," said Mal. "I can point out several."

That made all three of them laugh.

Mal's grin dropped away abruptly. "Hell's teeth, what's *she* doing here?"

Jessica turned to see a striking figure making her way towards them around the edge of the room. She wore the kind of white gown that never went out of fashion, a golden mask, and a mink half-cape. "Lucy!"

Tod squinted. "Who is she? I thought I knew everyone on the island."

"She's someone who usually stays in her bottle," growled Mal.

"She's an earth-born aspect of Avarice," said Jessica to Tod, "bound inside a perfume bottle. She's quite elderly, but powerful. Azrael has had her for a long time, and she acts like his mother."

Tod turned incredulously towards Jessica, and she leaned against his ear to whisper more softly. "She and Mal don't get along."

Mal had started purposefully toward Lucy. Jessica and Tod trailed after.

"Why is she out here now?" whispered Tod.

"No idea! I hope they're not going to fight."

Lucy stopped walking when she spotted Mal. She let him approach, giving him an appraising stare. Her eyes settled on his cat mask. "Subtle, Mal," she said in her cultured purr. "I almost didn't recognize you."

He ignored this. "I do not recall sending you an invitation."

"You didn't."

"Does this mean Azrael is here?" interrupted Jessica without much hope.

Lucy shook her head. "I just wanted a look at the debauchery. I confess, this is more tasteful than I expected."

"Give me a couple of hours," grated Mal. "This isn't your scene, Lucy." Jessica could tell that he meant, *"This isn't your territory."* These parties were Mal's particular province. For years, they'd been one of the few places where he was allowed to look human. Jessica liked Lucy and wanted her and Mal to get along. However, she could see how Lucy's presence—something Mal interpreted as hostile and judgmental—would feel like an invasion in this place.

"Does Azrael even know you're here?" demanded Mal.

Lucy's eyes scanned the crowd, the orchestra, the immense doors open to the beautifully lit garden. She said nothing.

"Gods, he is really just letting you wander around, isn't he?"

Lucy's eyes snapped back to Mal and now they were unmistakably hostile. "If you think so much of Azrael, perhaps you should trust his judgment. I live on this island, too. I have a right to know what goes on here."

Mal took a threatening step towards her. "Oh, I get it now. You're spying on me for your demon hunter! Are you his pet now, Lucy?"

"The only person here who could possibly be called a pet is you," she snapped, "you spoiled, overindulged lapdog."

Jessica sensed a thickening in the air as Mal and Lucy asserted their magical strength. It was an unpleasant sensation, like two overpowering odors in conflict. Mal described it as "arm-wrestling," but it felt like something more serious to Jessica. Tod probably couldn't sense it, but Jessica wanted to clap her hands over her ears. "Stop! Both of you just stop!"

Lucy took a step back. Jessica would have liked to think they were responding to her plea, but she suspected that, in fact, Mal had physically pushed Lucy away with his stronger magic. Jessica liked Lucy, but she didn't know what the older woman hoped to accomplish by sparing with Mal at the Revels of all places. This really was his territory.

Lucy straightened her narrow shoulders and gave a toss of her gleaming silver hair. Her voice came out cool and even again. "I'm going, I'm going. Gods know, I didn't expect a civil reception here. Good evening, Jessica."

Jessica frowned as Lucy moved away. She wanted to have a talk with Mal, but not here in the middle of a party with Tod watching them, and not with Mal so worked up. If he'd been a panther, he would have been bristling.

Is she really spying? Probably not. She probably just doesn't want to explain herself to him.

Jessica took a deep breath. "So...Capture the Flag?"

10

Azrael

Azrael was sitting at the kitchen table, reading in his silk dressing gown and slippers, when Mal and Jessica came clomping and chattering into the suite. Jessica was wearing a man's shirt and dress slacks, presumably borrowed from two different gentlemen, since they didn't match. The clothes were much abused and grass-stained. She was still wearing her pretty black boots, although they looked like they would need a brush and a polish. Her golden hair was half-unbraided with twigs in it, her cheeks flushed. She jumped up on the edge of the table, swinging her feet and grinning. "You waited up for us!"

Azrael put down his book and yawned. "Yes. It's only half past one. That's early for a Revel."

Mal lounged in the doorway, his jacket and waistcoat over one arm, his shirt half unbuttoned, his cravat wadded up and dangling out of one pocket. He had a few strands of grass in his dark curls. Azrael could tell that they were both slightly drunk on magic and alcohol.

"We played Capture the Flag in the hedge maze!" announced Jessica. "It was glorious! Also, Mal dropped the flag in the pool."

"Only because I wanted to see those lunatics jump in after it," drawled Mal. "They needed an excuse to take off their clothes anyway."

Azrael rose and stretched. "I trust you are both well-fed?"

"Exceedingly fed!" exclaimed Mal. "Completely fed! Pleased to give you magic in any orifice you desire."

Jessica snickered. "I have made friends. Mal has made conquests. Everyone had a good time."

Azrael plucked up a book from the pile on the table. "I found a new story I think you'd both like if you're not too sleepy."

There was a flurry of activity as they cleaned themselves up, salvaged what remained of their clothes, and got ready for bed. Fifteen minutes later, the three of them lay curled together, with an image of the night sky in the enchanted picture frame. Mal had turned back into a panther. He stretched out over the covers with his head on Azrael's chest, one paw extended over Jessica, who'd stretched out on her stomach beside them. The silver collar was digging into Azrael's sternum. He took it off Mal and tossed it onto the bedside table.

Azrael read them a story of love and war, set in the misty past before the sundering. He hadn't gotten very far before Mal's breathing grew deep and steady. Even Jessica couldn't seem to keep her eyes open. Her blond lashes kept fluttering shut. However, when Azrael muttered the word to turn out the lights, she woke up enough to thread her fingers through his. "Perfect day," she whispered.

Yes, he thought. *It really was.*

11

Azrael

Azrael woke in his big, empty bed as he always did. He rose, feeling a little foggy from a late night of work, but determined to rise early all the same and continue the preparations for his guests. He bathed and shaved, pausing to stare at himself for a moment in the mirror. He had a bruise on the side of his neck.

How did I do that?

The faint circle of mottled green and blue looked almost like…

Azrael felt dizzy. He put his hands on the edge of the sink. *I must have done it while I was working yesterday. A splash effect from a spell. I was concentrating. I didn't notice.*

He went to the bedside table and retrieved his magical focus—a necklace with heavy silver links. He put it on and used a tiny bit of magic to heal the offending bruise. An instant later, Azrael's pale skin looked smooth and unblemished. As it should. As it always did.

He donned one of his severe black suits, left his coat over his desk chair, and went into the kitchen to make breakfast and to read the book. The beautiful, beautiful book with its rich blue leather and embossed night sky. Azrael stared at it reverently while he poached an egg and made toast and tea. He studied the pages while he ate, delighting in his good fortune. He felt certain that this phenomenal artifact would make him the undisputed master of the Shattered Sea.

He considered the complex instructions. Then he went out to choose a location for the gate described in the text. *The gardens,* he thought. *The patio near the entrance to the hedge maze. That will do very well.*

Servants were coming and going in gardens, cleaning up some kind of party from last night. Azrael tried to remember what it had been about, then dismissed the question. *Anything to keep the courtiers pliant. After all, my creatures must be fed.*

There was a white flag on a stick floating in the pool. One of the groundskeepers was fishing it out. That reminded Azrael of something. He felt dizzy again and walked faster through the morning mist. *My domain,* he thought. *My creation. I am lord of the Shrouded Isle, and soon I will be Lord of the Shattered Sea.*

He reached one of several entrances to the hedge maze and paused, transfixed by a golden thread of hair on a branch. The world seemed to warp as though through a fishbowl. He couldn't breathe.

The next thing Azrael knew, he was in the great ballroom, speaking to his master groundskeeper. "I want the hedge maze completely cleansed from last night. Pristine, do you understand? Then I have a project that I will be conducting in the gardens. I do not wish to be disturbed."

He spent the rest of the morning addressing issues with his staff. Three guests would be arriving early. He would host a welcome dinner for them in the gardens. A larger group would arrive a few days after that. Their welcome feast would occur in the ballroom with the doors open to the garden.

"Will this dinner require couches, my lord?" asked his butler.

Azrael stared at him in confusion. "Couches?"

The butler adopted a tactful expression. "Will the guests be sporting, my lord?"

"Sporting what?"

The butler looked mildly put-upon. "Are you anticipating an evening of carnal delights, my lord?"

Azrael laughed. He couldn't have said why. The laugh ended in a kind of sob. "No." His head hurt. He needed to read the book. He needed to lie down.

12

Mal

Mal woke in a cold, foggy place. He thought he was outdoors: broken flagstones underfoot, something that might have been moonlight glowing through the drifting mist, everything utterly silent.

Mal stood, shivering. He was a panther. There was condensation on his whiskers. He saw that he'd been lying beside a stone fountain the size of a duck pond. Ink-black water churned within. At the center, a round platform, perhaps five paces across, rose out of the water. It looked like it ought to create a spray of water into the fountain, but it was dry. The platform was encircled by an ouroboros statue—a silver serpent, eating its tail. The water of the fountain moved in a slow vortex, as though the ouroboros were the center of a lazy whirlpool.

Something about the serpent made Mal's skin crawl. He stumbled backwards, off the flagstones, into wet grass. "Hello!" he shouted. "Azrael! Jessica!" His voice did not even echo. It was simply swallowed by the mist. *Where am I?*

Mal backed further from the statue and came up against a wall of thorny hedge. He turned and saw a corridor of deeply shadowed green. Mal circled the fountain with a sinking feeling. He found one corridor after another, but no clear exit. *I'm in some kind of maze.*

Mal shut his eyes, opened them again. *I'm dreaming.* But he knew that wasn't quite right.

Mal took a deep breath and did something he had not dared to do since he'd fled from his entity. He stretched his essence out into the fifth dimension, towards the astral plane. He should be able to do that easily. He was an unbound astral demon. The collar wasn't even around his neck at the moment. Reaching the astral plane should have been as effortless as twitching his tail.

Nothing happened.

Mal forced himself not to panic. *This is a nightmare. I'll wake up soon. All I have to do is be patient. This is a nightmare.* There was another possibility, but Mal didn't want to think about it.

He turned and plunged down one of the shadowy hedge corridors. *It doesn't matter which way I go. I'll wake up soon.* However, dream or no, he couldn't bear another moment beside the ouroboros.

13

Azrael

Azrael woke in his big, empty bed as he always did. As he would for all his days. He sat up and noticed markings on his oak headboard. The hastily scrawled words read: "Something is f"

Azrael put his finger out to touch the words, deeply puzzled. The handwriting looked like his own…if he'd been in a desperate hurry. He searched around in the pillows and found a discarded writing pen. Not a bone pen. Just an ordinary ink pen.

Azrael stared at the words. His head hurt. A thought came to him, seemingly at random: *Punishment and reward.*

He looked away from the strange scrawl, felt instantly better. He bathed, shaved, and dressed. His suite seemed so quiet. *I should enchant the picture frame to show the gardens, transmit birdsong.*

The frame showed nothing but smooth plaster at the moment. Azrael had a vague memory of having used it to… what? Visit pocket worlds? How long ago was that?

He had an urge to do so again. People in the pocket worlds would be safe to talk to. But why would he need to talk to anyone? He rubbed his eyes. He wanted to read. Not a textbook. Not even the delightful book on his kitchen table. A novel. He wanted to read a novel. To disappear into its pages, to get outside of his own head for just a moment.

Outside his own head…

Don't be ridiculous. You've no time for that now. You'll have time enough later. All the time in the world.

Azrael caught a glimpse of himself as he walked past the washroom mirror—dark eyes, pale skin, an intimidating stare, thin lips pressed into a fierce line, a flash of silver around his neck. Azrael touched the necklace that lay against his skin, his magical focus.

Collar.

Azrael blinked. A demeaning way to think of his focus. And yet that was the first word that had sprung into his mind when he looked at it. *My collar? No. Someone else's collar.*

Blinding pain behind his eyes.

Azrael crouched over, hissing with discomfort. He was suddenly filled with rage. He couldn't say why or at whom.

The other magicians. The enemies you've lulled into a false sense of security. Warmongers, power-hungry, murderers, self-righteous pricks. You're going to burn them all.

Azrael felt unsteady, but he straightened anyway. *Eat. I need to eat.* He made his way to the kitchen. As soon as he arrived, he forgot about anger, fear, and even hunger. Because there was the book. Of course! There was his reason for living. Such a spell it contained! Such a marvelous work of art. Everything made sense now.

Azrael sat and read. He lost track of time. Finally, he got up and went out to the gardens. They were pristine, without a trace of past frivolities. He ordered supplies brought, then went to his tower to get special ingredients.

The tower was a bit of a mess. Azrael remembered that he'd been working on a magical airlock up here. *But that won't be as important as I thought. My guests won't be here long enough for it to matter.*

He paused halfway across the room and frowned at a fine layer of salt he'd forgotten to sweep off the floor. In the middle of the salt, lay an enormous pawprint.

Azrael's skin prickled with heightened awareness, eyes darting around the room for a threat. He spoke a spell of revealing, but no monsters showed themselves. But dear gods, the thing that had made that print must be the size of a pony. *Did I summon something to help me yesterday? Or was that the day before?*

He rubbed his eyes. *I must have.*

"Did I leave handprints all over your body and pawprints all over your heart?"

"More like teeth marks all over my heart."

Azrael felt as though he were seeing double. He remembered those words, but he could not put them into context. *Did I say that? To whom? Why?*

Azrael felt like a drowning man who'd broken momentarily to the surface of the water. *This is not me. I am never confused. Something is wrong. Something is being done to me. I have to fight it. I have to remember… To remember… What?*

He was pacing around his tower, panting. And suddenly he wasn't sure why.

We need to hurry. Why did he tend to think of himself as "we"?

"*I* need to hurry," he said aloud. *I need to work on the spell. There will be many problems. Lots of problems to solve. I need to get everything necessary from my tower, because I don't want to come back up here. Too many distractions.*

Azrael seized the broom with shaking hands and swept up the salt. Relief washed over him as the pawprint disappeared. He'd probably been mistaken. It wasn't a pawprint at all, just a trick of the light.

He leaned over his desk to retrieve a vial of ambrosia and caught sight of the toad-owl skull where he kept his pens. To his great irritation, there was a crack in it. *My toad-owl!*

My...

"Mine, mine, mine."

The room was spinning. Azrael leaned heavily on the desk.

You belong to no one, whispered a voice in his head. *You are complete in yourself.*

Yes, of course that was true. Azrael of the Shroud belonged to himself and no one else. Ever since he'd escaped alone from the fires of Polois. Ever since he'd erased Laurence Crowley. Ever since he'd severed his last tenuous ties to the human race. Azrael of the Shroud needed no confidants, no peers, no friends, no lovers, nothing but his work. He belonged to no one.

The room had grown blurry. Azrael touched his face, felt a bewildering wetness.

He was suddenly tired, so tired. He needed to go lie down. He needed to read the book again. Then everything would make sense.

He felt calmer as he left the tower room, calmer still as he walked down the stairs, his arms full of supplies. However, as he stepped from the entrance, he found himself muttering over and over, "I need to remember, I need to remember, I need to remember… What? Salt? No, that wasn't it."

14

Jessica

Jessica woke to a complete absence of sensation. She'd felt this once before, when Azrael had used Lucy's one-way jump to take them from Faerie to the High Council courtroom in Bethsaria. The sense of utter void had only lasted a second—not enough time to panic, but enough time to give Jessica a healthy respect for magical traps.

This time lasted more than a second.

Jessica was blind and deaf, with no sensation of air or clothes against her skin, no sense of where her limbs were in space or even if she had limbs. She was a consciousness suspended in the void with no understanding of how she'd gotten there or how long it might last.

If Jessica had had a heart, it would have been hammering out of her chest. If she had had a voice, she would have screamed herself hoarse. If she had had a body, she would have thrashed. But she had only her thoughts, and those were going mad.

"Help me! Help me! Help me!"

She was an animal in a trap, and she had to escape, she *had* to. Then Jessica saw…something. A hole, a pinprick. The only way out. But it was too small or the wrong shape or the wrong direction. She could not get through it without turning herself inside out. And so, in desperation, she did.

15

Azrael

Azrael woke, walking beside the sea on a moonlit night. Fog was rolling off the land, but the sea breeze blew it away.

The shore. Azrael thought he recognized it. *Have I ridden here recently?*

He wasn't dressed warmly enough. He shivered. It did not occur to him to feel anxious, only vaguely annoyed. *Where am I?*

The land to his left seemed overgrown with a dense hedge. Now and again, he saw breaks—dark trails winding away inland. None of them looked inviting. That did not seem right, though the shore still seemed familiar. *Am I on my own island? What has happened here?*

The silence was profound. No night birds sang in the hedge, and even the noise of the surf seemed muted. At last, rising out of the mist, Azrael spotted a tumble of rocks. To his surprise, another man sat at the peak, staring out to sea.

Azrael stopped to contemplate this person. He'd gotten quite close in the drifting mist, silent in the fog and sand. The stranger obviously had not seen or heard Azrael's approach. He was a big man, broad-shouldered, well-muscled, but huddled over with one knee drawn up to his chin. He wore a shirt and trousers that looked too thin for this weather. Moonlight shone on skin the color of milk tea. A tangle of black curls blew around his head. He was a remarkably attractive man, Azrael thought, with a twinge of distraction, but he looked so sad. After a while, the man rubbed absently at his face and then dropped his forehead against his knee.

Azrael waited for him to sit up and look around, but he didn't. The stranger remained huddled for a long time, unmoving, and at last, Azrael cleared his throat. "Hello?"

The man's head jerked up. He stared down from the rocks through the drifting mist. "Azrael?" His voice cracked with emotion.

Azrael felt dizzy again. That voice...

Then the man was leaping down, stumbling through the rocks so quickly that Azrael was afraid he would hurt himself. It did not occur to Azrael until the man was on the ground and coming towards him to wonder whether this person might be dangerous.

Azrael backed away, saying the only thing he could think of. "Excuse me, you don't seem dressed for this weather..."

"Azrael!" thundered the stranger. His gem-green eyes had a bright sheen. "This is a spirit vessel, isn't it? You put me in a spirit vessel! Why? Why?" He caught Azrael by the shoulders and shook him. "What did I do? What did I do, Ren?"

Azrael was overwhelmed with feelings he could neither understand, nor tolerate. He shook himself loose and put several swift paces between them. The man did not attempt to follow, but dropped to his knees in the sand, weeping. "Was it your desk? The tower? I'm sorry! I'll never do it again. Or...if it was something else, please tell me. I'm sorry, I'm sorry..." He gripped his head with both hands, crumpling in on himself. "I hate being alone! I can't stand it. Please, please, please..."

"Who are you?" whispered Azrael.

The man raised his head slowly, his eyes huge in the moonlight. "Did you make yourself forget me?" he whispered. His great chest rose and fell as though he'd been something much smaller—a bird, a rabbit. His eyes darted this way and that. He looked like he was about to lose his mind. It was incredibly disturbing. If Azrael had known how to flee, he would have.

The stranger made a choking noise. "Gods." His despair was palpable. "You did. You put me in a spirit vessel. And then you made yourself forget."

16

Azrael

Azrael woke alone, screaming. "Mal!"

17

Azrael

Azrael came fully awake, sitting on the edge of his bed. He was very upset. He thought he'd had a nightmare, but he couldn't remember what it was about. He was breathing quickly, his heart beating too fast. He was sweating. *I need to get up and get to work. Lots to do today.*

No. I need to calm down. I need to…

"Remember," he said the word aloud and felt an instant jolt of pain in his head. He gritted his teeth. "I know something is wrong," he said to the empty room. He passed a shaky hand over his brow.

And found he was holding a pen. He stared at it. Then, slowly, he turned towards his headboard. That sentence had gotten longer: "Something is feeding"

Azrael's mouth went dry. Three words. He read them again. He curled over as the dizziness washed through him. He felt rung out, hollow.

So he did what he knew would make him feel better. He bathed and dressed and went out to eat something and read the amazing book. Then he went down to the gardens and recommenced work on his project. Azrael forgot about his nightmare. He forgot about strange words written over his headboard. He lost himself in the work.

He was eating his solitary lunch in a gazebo about midday, when one of the servants approached him—a freckled redhead. Azrael searched his memory for the young man's name. *Loudain. Thomas Loudain. Goes by Tod. Magician turned werewolf. His family number among my enemies, although I have gained their trust by agreeing to shelter this whelp. He will be a useful bargaining chip, but he may also be a spy. He must not be allowed to see the project.*

Azrael looked at the young man coldly. "Your services are not required here."

Tod bowed. "My lord, I'm sorry to trouble you, but…"

He hesitated, almost as though he expected Azrael to fill the silence. When he did not, Tod's eyes flicked up. He spoke in a near whisper. "Did you send them away?"

Azrael glared. He wanted to turn and see whether any of his supplies were in view of the gazebo. He wondered whether he should simply kill the young man and be done with it. "Did I send who away?"

Tod stared at him, confusion and something like fear playing across his face. "Jessica and Mal."

Azrael frowned. "Who?"

18

Azrael

Azrael woke in his bed. He was sitting on the edge again. He was wearing a rumpled suit. Apparently, he'd gone to sleep in his clothes. *Something is very wrong.*

Peace, whispered a voice in his head. *Be at peace. All is well. You have problems to solve, work to do.*

Azrael stared fiercely at the smooth plaster of the enchanted picture frame. "I am no one's puppet," he said to the air. "I know something is wrong, and when I find out who is doing this to me, I will *bury* them."

It's the other magicians. Your lifelong enemies. They are at fault. Murderous, meddling bastards. You must eliminate them. The world will be better off once you eliminate them.

Yes, of course it was their fault. Azrael relaxed. They'd done this to him—taken him in as a child only to use and abuse him, kept him friendless and isolated, ripped apart what little comfort he'd attained at the school with their deadly squabbles, left him homeless and alone as a teenager, hunted him as an adult, constantly searched for a weakness, called him to trial as a dark magician simply for eliminating a dangerous necromancer. They had honed him into the weapon that would destroy them.

I should call a demon, Azrael found himself thinking. *A sorcerer should always have one or two demons as a source of magic and for protection.*

You don't need a demon, silly. You have the book.

Azrael felt better. He got up and went into the kitchen. The blue leather volume lay open on the table. It was certainly a magical artifact of great power. He'd been taking magic from it each time he read, and there seemed to be no end to its stores. Azrael would not need a demon any time soon. He sat down and began to read.

He was startled when a woman walked into the room. Azrael stared at her—an older woman, richly dressed, well-groomed with tasteful cosmetics. She had aristocratic features—hooded eyes, high cheekbones, silver hair darkening at the tips. Her gown was white, her fur coat black, her jewelry gold.

Something clicked into place in Azrael's head, a door opening under pressure. "Lucy." He couldn't understand why he'd failed to recognize his dragon demon for a moment. He'd had her for years. Yes, of course. Lucy.

"My dear boy, you look dreadful!" Lucy was peering around the room with an expression of distaste. "Have you and your paramours decided to lock yourselves in and live on love? I realize you need to make up for lost time, but I do wish you'd give a good impression to the Council. I can show Jacob around myself, but Loudain and Lady S will expect you to play the gallant host."

Her words made no sense, and Azrael did not quite like her over-familiar tone. "I will dispose of those three fools on the night they arrive. They will be a test—an appetizer for my creature. That way, I can make any needed adjustments before the rest get here."

Lucy froze, staring at him. She started to say something, stopped. Her eyes went a little unfocused.

Azrael was annoyed. "Stop staring at my aura. I don't recall summoning you. Why are you here?"

She said nothing for a long moment. When she did speak, her words were carefully measured. "I did think you called me, darling. Something is certainly pulling on me. It's pulling very hard at the moment." Her eyes skipped to the book. They went unfocused again.

Azrael stood up. He felt unaccountably angry. "Well, I did not call, and I do not wish to be interrupted."

Lucy's eyes snapped back to sharp attention. She looked unsteady. "Did you say you are going to feed our guests to something?"

"Of course I am! Why else would I invite my mortal enemies into my stronghold?"

Lucy looked at Azrael as though she'd never seen him before. She spoke in a low, urgent voice. "Where are Mal and Jessica?"

Azrael felt a spike of pressure through his head like a warning shot. He screwed up his eyes. "Who? No, don't tell me; I don't care. I don't want you here right now. Please go."

"Beelzebub's tits." Lucy did not swear often, and the obscenity sounded strange in her cultured murmur. She took a couple of quick steps back and forth. "Fuck, fuck, fuck... You need an anchor." Her eyes snapped to his neck, saw the necklace. "If that was on Mal... But it's not. Because you two have been playing games. Fuck."

She bit her lip, jaw working. "It's going to get me, too. Because my bottle is open, and the moment I disappear, you'll forget I exist." Lucy shrugged out of her mink half-cape and threw it around Azrael's shoulders, the fur whisper-soft against his skin. She leaned into his face with terrible intensity. "This may not work, but it's the best I can do. Now listen to me: you are being played, master-of-mine. Someone is using memory magic on you. But nobody yet won a game of memory magic with Azrael of the Shroud. You are going to beat this thing. I have complete faith in you, dear boy."

Azrael frowned. Lucy's words still made no sense, but he felt a sudden rush of gratitude and something like comfort. "I—" he began, but Lucy talked over him.

"You will win this fight, Azrael. In the meantime, I am going to make sure you don't lose everything you value while you're getting your feet under you. We'll find out who did this." She shut her eyes and swallowed. "We'll find out before you kill Jacob." She said the last as though she was trying to reassure herself. "Because I don't believe it's him. I…" She swallowed. "No, I don't."

A confusion of images flicked through Azrael's head. Beautiful, ornamental carp, swimming beneath the mirrored surface of a lake. He'd been talking to Lucy there. And to someone else. Two other people? Azrael's hands clenched into fists. "Lucy, help me."

Her voice sounded equally strained. "Don't take the coat off. Use a charm or something. You should be able to do that. The script should allow that if it allowed you to keep the collar."

Before he could think what he was doing, Azrael plucked a strand of his own hair, twisted it with a strand of fur from the coat, and whispered the words that would bind them together. *Dangerous,* murmured a voice in his head. *Your own hair? This coat is not a coat. It is part of a demon.*

He ignored his own doubts. "Done," he said aloud.

Lucy smiled at him. "Good boy. You *will* win this. Now dismiss me. If it grabs me from outside my bottle, I'll be as useless to you as they are."

Azrael opened his mouth. *"Fly away home, my friend."* He'd dismissed a demon once with those words. Who? When? It felt important to remember, but he couldn't. With an effort, he managed, "Go back to your bottle, Lucy." He infused the words with magic—a true command.

Lucy turned like a person preparing for battle, and left.

19

Tod

Tod made beds, ran baths, cleaned, swept, and mopped. He carried food and clean clothes to beautiful rooms through sweetly smelling hallways, rich with soft tapestries, heavy carpets, mirrors, frescoes, and erotic murals. He spoke politely to courtiers and the handful of political guests currently on the island. He applied just the right amount of flirtation, as was expected in the sex-drenched atmosphere of a court designed to feed an incubus...or a fledgling succubus. It was a place perfectly tailored to meet their needs without causing lasting damage to humanity.

And now they were missing. And their master had run mad.

Tod tried not to panic as he turned the problem over in his mind. Azrael had responded without a flicker of recognition to the names of his two closest friends, his lovers. Mal, indeed, was practically a part of him.

He is suffering from some form of possession. It couldn't be complete possession. Azrael was functional enough not to alarm the servants, although they were certainly whispering that he was behaving oddly. He knew his way around his own domain. He was building something in the gardens, and he was very specific about the supplies he required. He hadn't asked for anything he didn't own, nothing truly bizarre. He spoke to servants by name. And that meant... *He's only allowed to remember what his attacker wants him to remember.*

Tod came from a long line of wizards. He'd had magic himself before the wolf bite. Tod couldn't *use* magic. Not after the wolf. But Tod knew *about* magic.

Could Mal be doing this? The thought sickened Tod, but he forced himself to consider it. Technically, yes. Demons, especially astral entities, could wear a human like a skin suit. *An incubus might even consider that the ultimate form of penetration,* whispered a nasty voice in Tod's head. Gods knew Azrael had dropped all his guard around his charming familiar. Mal could have taken possession of Azrael and consumed Jessica, just as a larger predator might consume a smaller one. Mal could then ride Azrael's consciousness without completely devouring him, allowing the sorcerer to perform the magic Mal required for whatever he was planning.

Tod shrank from that possibility. He did not want to believe anything so horrible had happened to Jessica. And besides… *Mal wouldn't do it.*

Even before Jessica's arrival, Tod would have laid odds that the incubus was attached to his master on more than a superficial level. That wasn't to say Tod trusted him. He would not have been surprised to learn that Mal had devoured his master in a moment of weakness or instinct, but this calculated cruelty, this long strategy game? *I cannot believe he would do that.*

But if it isn't Mal…

That might be even worse. Azrael was a memory specialist. He'd gotten very good at memory magic while cleaning up the misunderstandings, hurt feelings, and broken hearts that Mal left in his wake. For someone to get the better of Azrael with memory magic… *Gods, we are in a bad place.*

In spite of Tod's larger fears, one thought kept drowning the others: *I have to find Jessica.* Tod didn't know what to do about Mal—either to stop him if he'd gone bad or to help him if he was in trouble. But Jessica was Tod's friend, and they had looked out for each other in the past. Romantically, Jessica would never be more than a casual lover—a fact to which Tod had reconciled himself early in their acquaintance. But they were true friends, and they had each other's backs. If Tod had gone missing, he had no doubt Jessica would have done everything in her power to find him.

That would be easier for her, Tod thought wryly. *Jessica has the ear of the most powerful person on this island, and I do not.* Azrael had looked very unfriendly in the garden. *Whatever's riding him will not let him help me.*

Tod asked about her, of course—among the staff and the courtiers. No one had seen her since the Revels. Jessica had a lot of friends, but not many in whom she confided. She was the sort of person to whom people told their secrets, not the sort who did the telling.

Near noon of the next day, Tod got up his nerve to go to the unassuming wing where Azrael kept his simple rooms. He knew Azrael was in the garden, but that didn't mean the rooms were unwatched. Tod tried the door. Locked, of course. He knocked—softly at first, then more forcefully. At last, he threw caution to the wind and shouted, "Jessica! It's Tod; are you in there? Jessica!" Tod strained his ears, but the whole wing seemed profoundly quiet.

Screw it. Tod stripped right there in the hall, cursing every gilt button on his servant's livery. Then, he changed.

It was always painful, more so when he tried to go too fast. Muscles and bones broke, tore, reformed. There was always a moment in the middle when Tod didn't think he could bear it. He would just give up halfway—a deformed monster with its guts on the floor. Then, abruptly, the pain ceased.

Tod stood lower to the ground. The world beyond his eyes looked grayer, but the world beyond his nose and ears came alight. Scents for which men had no names bloomed into stories in Tod's mind. Vague, distant noises sharpened into focus. Azrael had left his rooms this morning with traces of salt and silver and horse on his shoes. The maid who stocked his pantry had come and gone. And there was Mal's scent. And there was Jessica's.

Tod sniffed all around the door and even grew bold enough to go to the end of the hall. Not many people came this way. Mal and Jessica's scents were easy to identify. They were also disappointingly old. Neither of them had been down this hall in three days, not since the Revels. Tod sniffed carefully under the door itself. He listened intently. *I don't think they're in there.*

He couldn't be positive, of course. Tod could think of all sorts of scenarios that would not have brought their scents or sounds to him from the depths of the suite. *But they're not just going about their business.* If they were in the suite, they'd been tightly confined.

It was one more piece of the puzzle, at least. Tod shifted back into his human form without being disturbed. He dressed and returned to more populous regions of the palace, thinking furiously. An idea had occurred to him, emboldened by his successful reconnaissance.

I'm a werewolf for gods' sakes. I can track damn near anything.

He would have to make some adjustments first, adjustments that frightened him, but Tod wouldn't let himself think about that. *It won't work anyway if I don't have something of hers.*

Tod felt amazed and a little sad to realize that he didn't have a single thing. He had had Jessica's clothes through his hands more times than he could count—her hair between his fingers, her tongue in his mouth. But he hadn't kept anything. He'd avoided that on purpose. When she'd written him letters sealed with spit, he'd told her to stop doing that—to use some other adhesive. Then he'd burned those envelopes to protect her. She was a magical creature. She had to be careful. Blood, hair, spit, fingernails—those things could be used against her.

The thought of the letters gave him an idea. *I wasn't the only person she wrote. Who else on the Shrouded Isle? Anyone besides Azrael?*

Tod didn't have to think about that for more than a second. *Yuli. She wasn't at the Revels. Gods, I hope she hasn't disappeared, too.* At least Tod knew where to find her room. At least it wasn't guarded by a possessed sorcerer.

20

Lucy

Lucy woke in moonlit fog on wet grass beside a hedge maze. Water whispered nearby. She sat up and discovered she was a dragon. *This thing—whatever it is—had to break us down into* magic in order to pull us inside. Poor Jessica. I wonder if she's even alive. Or sane.* Lucy tried an experimental shift into human shape and found that she was able. *That still works, at least.*

She returned to her dragon form because the dragon had a better nose for magic—the only scent that mattered here. She realized, with a grimace, that she didn't have a clear idea of Jessica's magical signature. She'd never really been exposed to it. Jessica had never tried to use magic on her. *Too polite, more's the pity.*

Lucy knew Mal's magic, though. She'd sparred with him more times than she could remember, and she knew the taste and smell of his magic intimately—dark chocolate and seduction and decadence. He'd paced all over the ground here, trampling the grass. He'd gone into the hedge maze at multiple points. He'd attacked it in a few places, ripping up the thorns, but doing no real damage.

"Yes, yes," muttered Lucy, "it's all about you, isn't it? I can't smell anything else, and gods, I wish you wouldn't pace so much. It's going to take me forever to figure out which way you went."

She crossed the clearing and ran up against something made of stone. Lucy raised her head and saw the fountain—the lazily moving black water, the silver ouroboros gleaming in the mist. She stared at it for a long beat, the tip of her golden tail twitching. She could feel its slow pull, its steady... *Digestion?* The eyes of the serpent seemed to laugh.

"Azrael is going to turn you inside out and break you down for parts," Lucy informed the fountain. Then she chose what she hoped was Mal's freshest scent trail, and glided away into the maze.

21

Tod

Tod was relieved to learn from the housemaid assigned to Yuli that she'd not gone missing. "She's been receiving meals in her room lately," said the maid. "She's not feeling her best." Tod knew better than to ask for details. Servants took the privacy of courtiers seriously.

Tod's duties kept him busy until after dinner. He didn't want to attract attention, so he waited. It was after eight o'clock by the time he arrived at Yuli's door. He'd knocked three times and was about to give up, when the door finally opened a crack.

A dark, almond-shaped eye peered out at him. The white looked a little red around the edges. "Yes?"

Tod swallowed. "Miss Yuli, I know you haven't been feeling well, but I need to speak to you. It's about Jessica. May I come in?"

Yuli opened the door wider. "Of course. What's wrong?"

Tod came into the room and waited until the door shut behind him. He'd never spoken much to Yuli. She was one of those girls who came to the Shrouded Isle for the experience, but never gave her heart to it. She was no prude, but she preferred sexual adventures with political guests who would not stay or become attached to her. When it came to her peers, Mal was right that Yuli preferred to watch. Her heart belonged to someone else, and she avoided any emotional entanglements. Tod respected that. But he'd avoided her for another reason.

Yuli's father was an inquisitor on the island next to Tod's family seat. Inquisitors made Tod extremely nervous. If any of them ever found out what he was, he would not be able to go home again even for a visit. So he'd avoided Yuli, and that wasn't difficult, because Yuli seemed just as happy to avoid Tod.

She stood in the middle of her beautiful suite now, wearing a pink silk dressing gown with embroidered sleeves. The color brought out the pink of her lips against her nut-brown skin. Her long hair made a dark ripple over her shoulders in the soft light.

Tod noticed a book open on her nightstand—a book he'd seen on Jessica's nightstand last week. *Of course they share books.* He also noticed an abundance of tissues, both on the bed and in the trashcan, along with numerous crumpled papers that looked like letters. He changed what he'd been about to say. "Are you alright?"

Yuli gave a self-deprecatory smile. "It's nothing. I think my boyfriend is breaking up with me, that's all." Her face crumpled, and she reached for a tissue with a helpless expression. "I'm sorry, I know it's stupid. What do I expect when I volunteer to spend four years on the Shrouded Isle, huh?"

Tod wanted to put an arm around her. "I know it happens, but it's still wretched."

She waved her tissue. "If he would just say so instead of saying everything else... But it's not your problem. Please tell me what's happened to Jessica. I've sent her three notes in the last few days. She didn't answer, and it sort of hurt my feelings. I know she's busy with all her..." Yuli stumbled over her words. "With Mal. But I didn't think she'd just ignore me."

Tod wondered how much Yuli knew about Jessica. He knew she didn't know that Jessica was a succubus, but the way Yuli's eyes flicked away from his face made Tod wonder how much Yuli knew about *him*.

He forced himself not to ask. "Jessica has been missing since the Revels. Lord Azrael is behaving strangely. I think I need to find her, and I need something of hers to do it—blood, hair, spit, that sort of thing. You have letters she sealed with her tongue, correct?"

Tod had thought carefully about how to frame this. He waited, letting Yuli fill in the blanks. "You think Lord Azrael did something to Jessica?" She looked at him, wide-eyed. "But Jessica didn't do anything wrong! It's that man, Tod! Mal! He is trouble. It's not Jessica. We have to tell Azrael..."

Jessica had mentioned Yuli's antipathy towards Mal before. Tod wondered if Mal twigged some instinct of her inquisitor ancestry. Something that whispered, "Not human, not human, not human..." *Let's hope she doesn't look too closely at me.*

Tod held up a hand. "I don't think it's Mal. Although it could be. The point is, I can't track her without a piece of her, and I don't have anything."

Yuli looked at him narrowly. "You're a Loudain... Do you have magic?"

"I can track her with magic, yes," said Tod. It wasn't exactly a lie, although Yuli would think he meant a spell.

"Will Azrael let you use magic here? Illicit magic could get you killed, Tod."

"I have my ways. Trust me?"

Yuli sighed. She went to her dresser and returned with several pieces of paper. She extracted the letters and held out the empty envelopes to Tod. "Can I help?"

Tod took the envelopes. "I'm afraid not. Thank you. As soon as I know anything, I'll send you word. In the meantime, I think you should stay in here and keep telling everyone you're sick."

Yuli gave him a watery smile. "Are you suggesting I continue to wallow?"

"Absolutely," said Tod. "Wallow like mad and be damned to anyone who tells you otherwise."

Yuli laughed. She followed him to the door.

Tod had his hand on the knob when she said, quietly, "You're the one she should have chosen."

Tod turned to look at her. "Excuse me?"

"Mal is a creep. I know I'm not supposed to say that, and Jessica is my friend, but she should have picked you."

Tod was not accustomed to being favorably compared to Mal, and it made him laugh helplessly for a moment. "Thank you. Jessica is not a fool, and there are…things I'm not at liberty to say. But thank you."

Yuli nodded, looking embarrassed. Tod reached out against his better judgment and squeezed her hand. "You've been very helpful. I'll be in touch." *If I survive.*

22

Lucy

Mal was not as easy to track as Lucy had hoped. He'd wandered all over the maze, which seemed to terminate in a beach if she went far enough. Unfortunately, Mal had waded into the surf. Lucy lost his trail in the water again and again. She hoped he hadn't been foolish enough to try swimming. *Has he never been in a spirit vessel before?*

Lucy grimaced. *He probably hasn't. Or he doesn't remember.*

Spirit vessels with an interior were usually a closed loop. However, most vessels included no interior at all and rarely something so extensive. *This is a very strange vessel.* It had deceived Azrael, Mal, and Lucy herself on close inspection.

It's a trap, obviously. The vessel snatches demons. Then it feeds their magic back to their summoner, who is under the delusion that he's accessing a magical artifact. It's meant to make him destroy his own support system. A serpent eating its own tail, indeed. *Well, it's bitten off more than it could chew with me. If I can just find that panicking idiot.*

Lucy wondered whether time was altered in the vessel. Minutes might pass like days. Or perhaps it only felt that way because of the endless twilit mist without changing patterns of sun, moon, or stars to mark the hours.

Lucy took to the air once, just see if the moonlight had a source. She didn't stay up for long, however. Within two wing beats, she was completely isolated in the mist, with nothing to see either above or below. She didn't want to lose the thread of Mal's scent by coming down in some new part of the maze. She was even more afraid that she might accidentally sail over the water and become lost with no place to land.

Lucy was sniffing around a pile of rocks on the beach when she heard what sounded like a child weeping. She'd heard no sounds except the whisper of surf for what felt like days, and the noise—any noise—was welcome. Still, Lucy proceeded with caution. The weeping did not sound like Mal. This spirit vessel was full of oddities, and she would not put it past the maker to include monsters.

Lucy came quietly around the jumble of rock, avoiding tide pools, peering into little caves. The keening echoed and carried. At last, she spotted something like a shadow, huddled in an alcove. In the shifting light and swirling fog, Lucy couldn't get a good look, even as she drew closer. She thought, for one moment, that the thing really was a child. Or at least that it had the shape of a child. She thought, in the next moment, that it had no shape at all. But it was certainly crying.

When she was ten paces away, Lucy gave up trying to guess and whispered, "Mal?"

The noise stopped as though cut with a knife. Lucy had just time to register his green eyes—a confusing moment when he was neither quite a cat nor quite man nor quite anything else—and then he barreled into her, human arms locking around her dragon neck. "Lucy!"

Mal was clearly out of his mind. He babbled incoherently, hiccupping sobs while he held her head too tightly for her to speak. "He threw me away, Lucy! He threw me away and made himself forget me! I don't know what I did! Do you know what I did? And I don't know what's happened to Jessica. Did he make her forget me, too? I can't stand being alone. I can't stand it! And there's nothing to eat, and my magic is draining away, and I'm going to die in here, and I don't know what I did wrong!"

Lucy tried to speak, but his grip on her head was holding her jaw closed. Rather than shake him off, she changed into human form. She was instantly reminded that she didn't have her coat. The next instant, she was essentially wearing Mal. "Calm down!" hissed Lucy. "Malcharius, calm down!"

"He doesn't want me anymore," whimpered Mal. "I wanted him so much I came back from the astral plane, but it only took a few weeks for him to decide he doesn't want—"

"He is not doing this!" exclaimed Lucy, trying to talk over Mal's wailing. "Have some faith in the man you say you love! Azrael is under an enchantment. He didn't put you here."

Dead silence.

Mal pulled away from Lucy, staring into her face. He blinked a few times. Lucy could see the wheels turning in his head. Very carefully, Mal let go of her shoulders and took a step back. *Now he's afraid. Which should have been his first response.*

Mal's eyes were huge and dark. "Are you going to eat me, Lucy?"

For the first time in their acquaintance, she could have. Lucy could see right through his essence in places—the faint moonlight shining through his body to the rock wall behind. The condition in which she'd found him made it obvious that he was having a hard time holding himself together in any shape. His clothes were the sort that he usually wore to bed—too thin for this weather, but he probably couldn't summon the energy to make better ones.

Lucy thought, *If I ate him and Azrael never remembered him, a lot of people would probably be better off.* Aloud, she said, "I kept Jacob from banishing you a month ago, didn't I?"

Mal said nothing. His too-bright eyes scanned her face. "Make it quick?"

Damn you. "Mal, stop being dramatic."

He gave a jittery laugh and hugged himself. "I can't. I'm dying. And one way or the other, Azrael doesn't remember me. I saw him here by these rocks. He looked at me like he'd never seen me before."

Interesting. "It's the dreamcatcher," said Lucy. "It's a spirit vessel that absorbs demons. Then it makes their master forget them and believe that the dreamcatcher is a magical artifact. He takes magic from it, but he's really taking magic from us. Since we have no way to replenish…"

"He kills us," said Mal miserably.

"There's more to it than that," said Lucy. "This is a very strange spirit vessel…if that's really what it is. It's giving Azrael instructions to build something that's supposed to devour the magicians who are coming to visit."

"Have I only been gone a few days, then?" asked Mal in wonder. "It feels like years!" He stopped as he processed what Lucy had just told him. Mal's eyes narrowed. "You came after me because of Jacob."

"I came after you because I had no choice!" snapped Lucy. "It grabbed me, too, because my bottle was open. But it took longer to get me, and," she added with a note of smugness, "it grabbed me from *inside* my bottle. A piece of me is still in there, which means I still have access to a source of magic."

Lucy shifted back into a dragon. "I've spent plenty of time inside spirit vessels. This one is beyond odd. I'd like to look around a little more. There might be a way out if the designer was overambitious. There might be a flaw." Mal perked up. Lucy turned away with a toss of her head. "Come on; we're wasting time."

23

Jessica

Jessica. She said the name to herself over and over, until it was just a series of sounds. *Jess… Jess… Jessica.* The word didn't mean anything. She wasn't sure why she kept saying it. *Thinking it?* Was she really saying anything? Could she? Did she have a mouth? Had she ever had a mouth? What was a mouth?

She was moving through a foggy wasteland of broken machines. The place smelled like sweetness and salt and smoke and ash. Buildings sagged in the fog—gutted and fire-blackened. A brilliant red and gold banner that had once stretched across a lane now hung from a single pole, trailing in the dirt: Lady Zersic's Land of Wonders.

Jessica sniffed at the banner. She knew all the letters, and she thought she was making them into words, but she didn't know what the words meant. More distressingly, she didn't know whether she *should* know what the words meant.

She looked up and saw a circle of metal scaffolding looming high above her in the gray sky. Images flashed through Jessica's head: riding in something like that with her little sister, salty flavors, loud music, laughter.

Sister? She repeated that word to herself over and over. *That's a kind of person. Am I a sister?*

She wandered on through the empty lanes murmuring, "Sister" and "Jessica" and once, "Mal... What is a Mal? Is that a kind of person, too?"

The world was peaceful, quiet. Jessica thought she might lie down and sleep. Or perhaps not sleep exactly. Perhaps just lie down and watch to see if anything would happen. She could be patient for a long time. Perhaps forever. She didn't have anywhere to go, anything to do, anyone to be.

Jessica was startled by a beam of light across the lane ahead. It was shockingly bright and out-of-place. Jessica moved towards it warily. The light came from the door of a building. It was gutted inside, just like the others, but unlike them, it had an opening in the floor. The light was shining up from below.

Curious, Jessica started down the steps. She didn't like going headfirst, but she didn't seem to have a choice. She was suddenly baffled by her own body. It was not right. She knew that. But she had no idea what "right" might be.

The basement was not large. Jessica's nose told her that it contained mostly potatoes. Amongst the potatoes stood a narrow bed and a wide desk, covered in clutter. Two lamps burned in the room.

A person sat at the desk, hunched over a book, writing. Jessica remained on the stairs, well off the floor. She leaned into the room, sniffing. Beneath the earthy smell of the potatoes, she caught the odors of blood and salt and a sharp, astringent smell that her senses registered as magic. Her nose told her that the person was male, probably young.

He stopped writing abruptly and spoke without turning around. "Who's there?"

Jessica cocked her head. She didn't know how to respond or whether she should. *That was a question, right? You're supposed to answer questions.*

He turned. Jessica had an impression of dark, shaggy hair and eyes that looked too big in a hollow face. He was all arms and legs as he stood up, unfolding out of the chair. "What the hell?"

Jessica tried to back up the steps. That seemed harder than it ought to be.

"What the hell?" repeated the man—the boy, really. Then he laughed. Jessica did not much like his laugh. "You must have come out in the wrong place. Interesting. Can you even understand what I'm saying?"

Jessica took another step backwards, but the boy made a motion with his hand, and the cellar door shut with a boom that made her jump. *I don't like this, I don't like this, I don't like this!*

"Well, can you?" repeated the boy.

Jessica crouched down with a whimper.

The boy stuffed his hands in his pockets. "Huh. Well, you're awfully cute, but I need all the magic I can get right now. If the void wiped your memory, I might as well take what's left of you." He raised his hands. Then a monster came through the cellar door.

24

Tod

Tod had been bitten by a werewolf when he was seven years old. He remembered the event—remembered the panic and pain. However, he did not remember being an uninhibited werewolf, because his family had taken him to Lord Azrael before the next full moon.

Azrael's first act as Tod's new guardian had been to provide him with an inhibitor charm. The charm did not prevent him from changing shape, but it did make the change more difficult and more painful. It prevented him from changing by accident, in a fit of childish rage or anxiety. It also prevented him from losing his mind at the full of the moon. It did not prevent him from feeling unwell during that time, but he was not overcome with bloodlust. Since Azrael was the maker of the charm, its effects were strongest in his own domain behind his own wards. Tod hardly felt the changing moon when he was on the Shrouded Isle, whereas he was keenly sensitive to it when he went to visit his family.

Unfortunately, the inhibitor also blocked some of the positive aspects of being a werewolf. Tod was easier to kill while he retained the charm. It slowed his swift healing. His transformation was more painful. The supernatural keenness of his wolf-senses was blunted.

These were some of the reasons that rogue werewolves didn't like to be saddled with inhibitors. They called the charms "muzzles" and resisted attempts by law-enforcement to have the charms placed. The tendency of werewolves to resist safety restraints was one of the reasons that the Emerald King had simply declared werewolves monsters that must be put down for public safety.

Tod had always been a "good" werewolf. He'd retained his charm faithfully over the years. Everyone assured him this was for the best. Tod had never gotten a taste of life as an uninhibited werewolf. He didn't know what that felt like.

But he did know how to get rid of his inhibitor. He'd done it by accident a couple of times when he shifted. Naturally, the charm was nothing so simple as an object under Tod's skin like Jessica's birth control. The werewolf inhibitor had to be swallowed.

Tod's bedroom was one of the loft compartments high in the eaves of the palace, looking out towards wooded hills. It was a cozy room, not as ornate as the courtier's suites, but that was how he liked it. Tod stood naked in the middle of the room now and *focused*. He concentrated on that thing inside him which was not quite right—something alien that didn't belong. Then he changed.

The wrenching pain drove him to his knees, but Tod kept his attention focused on that deeper point of irritation—the thing which was not part of him. The pain grew unbearable. His guts were turning themselves inside out…and *there*. There it was. *Now!*

Tod came to his feet as a wolf, retching. He gagged up bile and then something that burned fiercely in his throat. Tod opened his eyes. A silver medallion the size of a large coin lay on the floor of his room in a puddle of vomit. The medallion was etched with runes and smelled intensely toxic to his wolf senses.

Well, that's done. He shivered. *Now I'm* really *breaking the rules.*

Tod hopped up on his bed next to the handful of envelopes that Yuli had given him. He sniffed them, carefully tweezing the smells apart in his mind. Even with the inhibitor charm, Tod was an excellent tracker. He had a good nose for ordinary scents.

Now, however, he could smell Jessica's magic—the trace left by her saliva. Jessica's magic was subtle. It made him think of wonder and curiosity and something that he could only describe as "bravery."

Tod curled up on his bed and focused on imprinting the magical odor on his senses. *I'm coming, my friend. I will search this whole island, and wherever you are, I will find you.*

But the time was still early by the standards of the Shrouded Isle—not even ten o'clock. Tod waited for the dead of night when Azrael's kingdom would sleep. While he waited, he dozed.

25

Lucy

Mal and Lucy walked the island. It wasn't large, but the hedge maze made it impossible to cover quickly. Because the maze had so many entrances, one could not perform the simple trick of always turning in the same direction. The maze dead-ended and looped and formed elaborate twists that dumped them back onto the beach again and again.

Mal seemed desperate to talk. He answered all of Lucy's questions with a flood of detail. No, he had not found any structures on the island aside from the fountain. The island's shoreline reminded him of the Shrouded Isle, but was not identical. Yes, Mal really had seen Azrael on the beach. "He came walking out of the mist, and I was so relieved. I thought he'd tell me what I'd done to make him angry. I thought I could fix it. But then he didn't know who I was, and after a few minutes, he disappeared."

"Disappeared?" echoed Lucy. "He didn't walk away? He vanished?"

"It seemed like that to me," said Mal. "I ran after him, but there was no trace, not even a scent."

"I wonder…" Lucy licked her lips. "We all thought the book was a dreamcatcher. What if we were sort of right? What if it's a dreamcatcher that's been modified? We're not technically in a spirit vessel, but a kind of pocket world?"

Mal frowned. "A permanent dream space? That would require a lot of on-going magic just to hold it together. It would require…one hell of a dream-walker among other things. Do you have any idea who's doing this?"

Lucy shook her head. Reluctantly, she admitted, "It almost has to be one of the magicians coming to visit."

Mal's tail lashed. "Such as your precious Jacob?"

Lucy rolled her eyes. "Such as any of them who'd like to get rid of the others."

"I knew we shouldn't have invited those assholes onto our island!"

They had arrived at the clearing around the fountain, and Lucy was grateful for the distraction. They circled the structure warily, sniffing. Lucy felt certain this was the source of the slow magical drain that she was beginning to feel in her own body and which had already taken a toll on Mal.

After a moment's consideration, Lucy slid the tip of her tail into the slowly churning water. She felt no pain, nor even any wetness, but when she lifted her tail, the tip had vanished as though cut with a knife.

Mal shuddered. "I'm glad I didn't try swimming."

Lucy regenerated her tail-tip with annoyance. "Well, now we know for sure that it eats magic."

"Let's get away from it," said Mal. "I feel like it's watching us."

Lucy looked at the statue thoughtfully. "I haven't given up on finding a crack in its armor. Let's keeping looking. Anything that isn't part of the pattern could represent a flaw."

They started back down a row through the mist.

"What if Azrael was dreaming?" said Mal. "What if that's why he showed up here?"

"Did you *just* figure that out?"

Mal ignored her. "If it's pulling on magic. It's probably pulling on his, too. It can't break him down into magic to get him through the portal, so it only gets him in his dreams. But...for him to look me in the face and not know who I am... What if it's permanent? What if..." Mal stopped walking. He turned to Lucy with a horrified expression. "Jessica can't change shape! Did it get her, Lucy? Was she in the suite?"

"I don't know, Mal."

Mal began walking faster and faster. "If she got stuck in between, she'd be in the void. She wouldn't know how she got there or how long it will last or whether she'll ever get out. She'll be so afraid. She might lose her mind!"

"Mal!" Lucy's dragon head shot out in front of him. "You are wasting energy. Energy is magic here. You cannot afford that. We don't know where Jessica is. Speculating is pointless. She may be fine. She may not. There is nothing you can do for her right now except look for a way out of this vessel or pocket world or dream space wherever the hell we are!"

Mal did not appear to be listening. "It's my fault. I made him break the seal too fast."

"What seal?" demanded Lucy.

"In his tower, he broke the encryption charm on the dreamcatcher, and we were... Oh, gods and he took down his wards!"

Lucy gave a huff, creating a tendril of steam in the wet air. "Stop giving yourself so much credit. Your cock isn't *that* magical. Azrael probably activated the damn thing when he broke the seal. It would have happened no matter how he broke it." Almost to herself, Lucy continued, "And that's hellish clever. Only a sorcerer worth trapping could activate the trap." She gave Mal a look of pure acid and added, "I suppose he wasn't paying the closest attention?"

Mal swallowed. "Not as such."

Lucy folded and refolded her wings. "Well that's done, and there's nothing we can do to change it. Let's comb this island for a flaw. Let's do it without panicking or wasting our strength."

26

Azrael

Azrael drew runes in spelled chalk on the flagstones at the entrance to the hedge maze. It was a laborious process. The runes had to be perfect. *Take your time,* he told himself. *Take your time to get it right.* On a deeper level, he thought, *Take your time to think.*

He'd given up trying to address whatever was bothering him head-on. If he started avoiding his work, voiced his concerns aloud, or questioned the servants, he'd just end up back in his bed with no memory of how he got there or what he'd done in the meantime. When he was calm and working, however, his thoughts became clearer.

Azrael ticked off things that did not make sense. He had a closet full of clothes that were not his own, items in his washroom that did not belong to him. He was having these strange black-outs. There had been other strange things. He was certain of that, but he could not remember them. Azrael had a vague, but urgent sense that he had lost something of great value.

Someone is performing memory magic on me.

Extracting one's self from a memory trap was difficult, but not impossible. Memory charms were never perfect. They worked best on a small scale. Azrael could easily make someone forget a name. People did that on their own all the time. A good magician could make a room full of people forget the details of an evening, particularly among companions they did not know and would never see again. He could erase an isolated event that was unconnected to other parts of a person's life, or he could alter small details of that event.

Large scale memory magic was much harder. Major events and complex personal relationships spread tendrils through a person's life. Erasing them left gaping holes that people tended to notice. Magicians attempting large scale memory magic could not possibly concoct a sufficiently convincing backstory to explain all of this to their victim's internal satisfaction. Instead, they usually employed techniques that encouraged the victim to do the explaining themselves—to concoct their own alternate version of events. These false histories must encompass unavoidable facts, but allow for the script that was being magically imposed upon them.

Such concoctions rarely held up to scrutiny. People realized that something was wrong. They were then faced with the daunting prospect of distinguishing real memories from false ones. A person who did not understand what was happening might easily lose touch with reality and go mad.

Azrael scowled at the rune he was drawing. A victim of memory magic usually cherished a set of underlying false assumptions that resisted the victim's inspection. There were usually obvious flaws in the script. These flaws could sometimes trigger an unraveling of the spell if the victim could identify them.

Remember what you can't remember. Gods know I've done it to other people often enough.

Yes, but I did it for good reasons, he told himself, *and whoever is doing this to me is obviously a fiend.*

Azrael tried to review his basic underlying assumptions about his life. He'd been orphaned by plague at a young age and taken in by a magical school where his gifts were not identified. He'd been little better than a slave to the children of wealthy magicians, who mistreated him. Then his abusers fought among themselves, destroying the school and killing his few friends. He'd escaped to wreak havoc on the opposing armies with his newly discovered talents. All records of his existence had been extinguished. Nobody knew his name.

Except that necromancer from this summer. The necromancy itself had been a ruse to get Azrael's attention and tempt him into the Shadow Lands. The magician had been a student from the school who'd escaped by locking himself inside a spirit vessel and taking over the unfortunate antiquities collector who'd opened the vessel decades later.

Azrael considered those events. *The necromancer made a frost bear golem in the Shadow Lands. It hunted me. I destroyed it with...* Azrael felt a twinge of discomfort and mentally backed away from the idea. But he took note. *Those events contain a clue that the script won't let me see. Very well. I'll find another way.*

In any case, he'd killed the necromancer and then gone to the High Mage Council's humiliating trial. They had accused him of dark magic. However, he'd weathered their inspection and managed to procure their goodwill. They were coming to visit him on the Shrouded Isle—to spy, no doubt, or to figure out how to steal his secrets. But Azrael was ahead of them. He would use their greed to make an end of them once and for all, doubtless saving the lives of their countless future victims. The Shattered Sea would be safer and more peaceful with fewer magicians.

Azrael licked his lips. That was correct, wasn't it? It felt correct.

One of them is probably doing this! One of the other magicians might be trying to stop him or cause him to make a mistake. One of them was surely the source of the memory charm.

But I have lost something, persisted a mournful voice in the back of his head. *I have lost something precious. And nothing I know explains this.*

Azrael sat back on his heels and flexed his fingers, resting them for a moment from the intricate rune-work. The fall air was cool, and he slid his hands absently into his coat pockets. *Why am I wearing a fur coat?*

He glanced at his shoulders. It was a half-cape. Azrael felt the script wobble, and he grasped desperately at the flaw. His fingers touched cold metal in the pocket of the cape.

I put the cape on this morning. He remembered. *I charmed it to remind myself not to take it off. Someone gave it to me. Someone...*

Azrael growled at the pain in his head. He was thinking too hard. He was not working.

He drew his right hand out of his pocket to see what he was holding. Two silver rings. Azrael stared at them as though mesmerized. Abruptly, he shoved them back into his pocket. *Before I set them down. Before I forget them.*

He got to work on the runes again, thinking. *I put the fur coat on this morning for...for some reason I thought was important at the time. And I changed out the contents of the pockets with my other coat. I remember doing that. The rings were already in my pocket. Why?* It felt terribly important to remember.

27

Tod

Tod came to his senses with the strangest feeling of dual reality. He knew he was still curled on his bed. He could feel his own doggy chin on his doggy paws. But he was also looking around…looking down at himself on the bed.

Does this always happen to uninhibited werewolves?

He could smell Jessica's magic—the clever, playful, curious scent of her nature. *Of course I can,* he reminded himself. *I'm lying with my nose right beside the envelopes.* Only now…

Now he knew how to follow it.

Tod blinked with eyes he did not truly have. He was seeing double—a foggy landscape super-imposed over his bedroom. *It's a dream,* he told himself. *I'm dreaming.*

But that's where she is, whispered the sure voice of the wolf. *That is where her trail leads.*

That doesn't make sense, thought Tod, but he took a step out of his body, into the foggy world of the dream. Instantly, his bedroom became a little dimmer, the desolate dreamscape more concrete. Jessica's scent became stronger.

Tod stopped asking questions and let his instincts take over. He was a hunter, running on a scent. It led through a landscape of burned out buildings, dilapidated tents, gutted merry-go-rounds, debris-strewn racetracks, and a skeletal Ferris wheel.

This was a circus, thought Tod. *It's a burned out circus. What creepy dreams you have, Jessica.*

Tod assumed he was in her dream. Nothing else made sense. *If I can find her, maybe I can get her to tell me where she is in real life.*

Tod passed a fallen banner that read: Lady Zersic's Land of Wonders. *I've heard of this place. It was controversial.* He couldn't remember the details. *Did Jessica visit at some point?*

He came around the corner of a lane and saw light through a doorway ahead. Tod reached it in seconds with his long, loping run. He peered inside, saw a destroyed toy shop. The light was coming from an open cellar entrance.

As he approached the stairwell, Tod noticed another scent. He'd been concentrating so fiercely on Jessica's that he hadn't really thought to search for other magic, but it was overwhelming here. It made him think of cold iron and fog and intricate gears.

Tod heard someone swearing—a male voice, rough with adolescence.

Tod peered downward. The cellar was well-lit, although he couldn't see much apart from the stairs and sacks of potatoes at this angle. His entire attention focused on a fluffy red fox, standing halfway down the stairs, looking into the room. The fox had hunkered down. Its ears and tail were low—clear signs of anxiety. Tod's breath caught. *Jessica?*

The adolescent voice spoke again. "You're awfully cute, but I need all the magic I can get right now. If the void wiped your memory, I might as well use what's left of you." To Tod's horror, the cellar door slammed shut.

Tod only hesitated for an instant. Then he went *through* the door. Tod understood in that moment why werewolves resisted inhibition. The door splinted around him like matchwood. It might as well have been tissue paper. The thrill of effortless destruction was glorious.

In the room beyond, a young man with an atrocious haircut and wispy beard stood gaping up at him, hands spread. The fox had plastered herself against the wall, bristling. Tod was almost certain that Jessica *was* the fox, but he bellowed her name anyway.

The fox's ears perked up. It was not quite the response Tod had been hoping for, but it was enough to satisfy him. Tod whipped down the steps, snatched up the fox like a puppy, and flashed out of the basement just as the young sorcerer recovered himself enough to cast some sort of binding spell.

Tod's legs locked.

But only for an instant.

That might have worked on a demon, he thought smugly. *But I am not a demon. Turns out, werewolves are better at a few things after all.*

28

Lucy

Lucy had truly believed she and Mal would find a flaw in the trap. This dreamscape was too elaborate, too large, too solid. It was overambitious. Lucy was well-acquainted with the tendency of magicians to overreach themselves. This seemed like an overreach. Yet she and Mal found nothing except for endless hedge, foggy beach, and the malevolent fountain.

Mal's babble of conversation ceased. He made disjointed remarks about Jessica and Azrael, but even those grew further apart. He had developed an alarming degree of transparency. He started to shiver, though he didn't seem conscious of it.

At last, Lucy said, "I could try to light a fire on the beach. Everything is wet, but I could try."

Mal didn't argue.

The fire took some finesse with a combination of human and dragon ingenuity, but Lucy finally managed to coax a pile of branches into a blaze. It gave off a gratifying amount of warmth. Mal stretched out beside the fire with his head on his paws. Lucy chose to sit in her human form, warming her chilly fingers.

After a bit of thought, she transformed her ball gown into a cream-colored sweater and a full, dark blue skirt. She considered trousers, but discarded that idea. *No need to become vulgar just because I'm in a demon-eating dream trap.* She wondered whether it was possible to sleep in this place. She was beginning to suspect that it wasn't.

They were quiet for a long time. At last, Mal said, "Why didn't you let Jacob banish me?"

Lucy frowned into the flames. *The truth makes me look weak. A lie makes me look weaker.* "Azrael was so happy…that morning when he came out to send me into the city ahead of the rest of you. He was…glowing. I just couldn't."

Lucy had expected an oration on Mal's abilities to produce glowing happiness, but Mal only raised his head to peer at her with fever-bright eyes. "Really?"

"You know it perfectly well," snapped Lucy. "I don't need to tell you what you do best."

Mal licked his lips. "Well…good. *I* was happy. I'm glad he was." Mal dropped his head on his paws again. "Jessica didn't deserve this. Maybe Azrael and I had it coming, but she didn't. She was kind to everyone, but she…understood me. Ren was mine, but he never understood me. And that was alright, because she did. She wanted some things I couldn't give her. I wish she'd gotten to have those things."

Lucy rolled her eyes. "You really do not handle solitude well."

"No," agreed Mal, "I really don't. I also don't handle dying well; I realize I'm not doing it very gracefully."

Oh, for fuck's sake. "Mal, I do not believe this thing will beat Azrael. I know it's difficult to wait and not be able to do anything, but please have a little faith and a little patience."

Mal didn't seem to be listening to her. "I was *happy*, Lucy. I waited all my life for it, and then I had it for a few weeks. And it was worth everything…worth coming back from the astral plane, worth never going home. I didn't know it would be so short, though. I suppose everyone feels that way in the end no matter how long they get to be happy."

"Mal."

He finally growled at her. "Can't you let me mourn them for just a moment? I know you've never liked me, but can't you listen for just a moment, since you're the only one to hear?"

"Mal." Lucy stopped trying to keep the softness out of her voice. "Come here, dove."

He blinked at her across the fire.

Lucy patted her lap. "Come on." When he still hesitated, she added. "I'm an old lady; lap cats are traditional."

He came, then, slinking around the fire, and hesitatingly rested his enormous head in her lap. Lucy stroked his nose and ears. To her surprise, Mal heaved a sigh that broke into a desperate, ragged purr. "You never call me dove," he muttered. "You call everyone else dove."

"Do I?"

Mal started licking her fingers. His tongue was strangely soft for a cat—wet, muscular velvet. "Enough of that," said Lucy, and Mal subsided at once.

After a while, he said, "Lucy, does your bottle have an inside?"

We've known each other for over a decade, and you've never once asked me that. "No. It's void, but it's easy for me to sleep there. It doesn't frighten me like it used to."

Mal shuddered.

"I'm a dragon," continued Lucy. "Avarice is not a social creature. Not like Lust."

"I would rather endure anything than be alone," whispered Mal.

"I know," said Lucy. *You're so desperate for closeness right now that you're willing to admit weakness even to me.*

"Lucy, do you love Jacob?"

Lucy was caught off-guard again. She hesitated. "I don't know, Mal. I met him a long time ago. We've been on opposite sides in the past, but that's just because my masters were at odds with him. He's…complicated."

Mal smiled, and Lucy felt strangely relieved. Mal in a state of grief was such an alien creature that Lucy wasn't sure how to respond to him. "Terrible taste in men?"

"Unequivocally."

"You're not keeping him around just because he could banish me?"

"No, Mal. That is just an added bonus."

He snickered. "Why do you hate me, Lucy? When we're telling jokes, it almost seems like we're friends."

"I don't hate you, Mal. You may infer this by my reluctance to see you killed."

"Yes, but you don't *like* me."

"I worry about Azrael. He's a well-intentioned young man with a lot of power. You are uniquely positioned to destroy him."

She'd expected a flurry of protests: I love him. I would never hurt him. Haven't you noticed all the sex we've been having, and I haven't eaten him yet? He's happy. You said so yourself.

But Mal didn't say any of that. Instead, he whispered, "Do you still think he would have been better off if he hadn't summoned me?"

Lucy shifted on the sand. "You *are* feeling morose."

"I'm dying."

"Stop saying that."

"But do you think he would have?"

Lucy screwed up her face. "If he'd summoned something else—something he wouldn't have fallen in love with, something he could easily dismiss when he no longer needed it? I don't know, Mal. I'd like to think he would have found human companionship, that he wouldn't have spent years pining for something that was all but unattainable, that he wouldn't have been so terrified of intimacy, so lonely. I'd like to think he would have had more friends—ordinary friends—because he wouldn't have created such immense emotional barriers to protect himself from you.

"But truthfully? I don't know. Azrael was a poorly adjusted teenager with a vengeful streak, no mentors, and more power than he knew what to do with *before* he summoned you. Maybe he would have become something worse if he hadn't known what it was to love another creature…even a dangerous, inhuman creature."

Mal had been honest, and Lucy was doing her best to be honest in return. Perhaps that was why she added, "I suppose I don't trust love. Love doesn't always save you. It doesn't always lead you in the right direction. It isn't always enough."

Mal's eyes flicked up from her lap. He didn't say anything, just watched her face. Lucy took a deep breath. Then she told him the story that she never told anyone. Because they were sitting beside a fire on a beach in a dream world from which she might never escape, and suddenly she wanted someone else to know.

29

Tod

Tod's euphoria vanished when he realized that he didn't know where he was going. He ran until they flashed through the sagging gates of the gutted circus. At that point, the fog became thicker. Tod felt grass beneath his paws, but it quickly thinned into something like clay. He didn't see any shapes in the fog—nothing at all beyond the circus walls.

What happens if I go past the edges of the dream?

In his mouth, the fox whined. Tod stopped running. He went back to the wall of the circus—a high wooden structure—

and followed it in the fog for a while. He listened for footfalls or voices, any sound of pursuit, but all was quiet. At last, he set Jessica down. She hadn't struggled or made any noises apart from that whine. Her silence was beginning to bother him.

"Jessica?" said Tod the moment she was out of his mouth. "Jessica, it's Tod. I'm sorry I had to carry you that way. I'm sorry I haven't let you see me like this before. I'm sorry if I scared you. Are you alright? Where are you in the real world?"

The fox looked up at him. In most respects, she looked like any other red fox with a white mouth, chest, and tail tip. She had black ears and black socks, thick fur, a flame-red coat. However, the fox's eyes were a startling blue. Jessica's blue.

Tod wanted to hug her. "Jessica, what happened to you?"

She just looked at him.

Fear crept in to smother Tod's relief. "Jessica?"

Her ears perked. She made another whine—one with far more vowels than any dog's. It was a noise peculiar to foxes. But no words.

Tod swallowed. "Jessica, has something really bad happened?"

She cocked her head, listening to him with keen attention, as though the sounds he was making were fascinating nonsense.

Tod kept talking to her. She kept listening. He couldn't tell whether any of it got through. At last, he leaned down and just licked her face—doggy comfort that might at least be understood. The fox leaned into him at once, her tongue flicking over his muzzle. She scooted forward and curled up against his front legs.

Tod wanted to weep. "Oh, Jessica, what's happened to you?"

He kept telling himself that this was just a dream. Perhaps Jessica always turned into a fox in her dreams. Perhaps she turned into a wild fox who couldn't understand words. Perhaps.

But Tod didn't believe it. *Something is horribly wrong.* He felt alone, inadequate to the situation, helpless.

Tod sat there for what seemed like an eternity with the fox snuggled against his legs. At one point, his vision blurred and he felt, for just a moment, the sensation of a comforter under his paws, the smell of paper beside his nose. *No! Don't wake up!* He stood very still and focused on his breathing. The sensation subsided.

Tod didn't think he'd be able to remain asleep come morning, though. "Jessica, if I disappear, you need to stay here. Stay where I can find you. Don't go wandering around the circus where that sorcerer might see you. Do you understand? Stay right here."

She looked up at him. He could not tell whether she understood.

Damn it. "How do I take you with me? Where *are* you, Jessica?"

At that moment, Tod heard a sound—the first new voice he'd heard in what felt like days. Someone was calling at a great distance. Tod didn't think he would have heard the voice at all without his canine senses. The voice was coming, not from the circus, but from the rolling fog. Tod pricked up his ears and concentrated.

He got to his feet. "Jessica, I think you should stay here." *If something bad happens, I can wake up. But I'm not sure you can.*

He turned to her and gently pushed her against the wooden fence with his muzzle. He held her there for a moment. "Stay here," Tod repeated. "I will come back. I promise."

Tod tore himself away before he could lose his nerve and loped into the fog towards the voice. He looked back once and was relieved to see the fox still sitting beside the fence, watching him.

Tod focused his entire attention on tracking that thin sound through the gray emptiness. The ground beneath him changed from clay to something smoother and slicker. Soon, he was running on what felt like air. Another sound joined the voice—a sighing noise. Tod's nose registered salt. Then he hit the water.

30

Azrael

Azrael came to himself, walking along a foggy beach. He had a vague sense that he'd been here before. Something was wrong. He needed to remember something.

He slid his hands into the pockets of his coat. A mink cape. *Lucy!*

Azrael stopped walking, running his hands over the cape, turning around, trying to see the whole thing without taking it off. *This is Lucy's. This is part of Lucy. How did I end up with it?*

"You need an anchor."

Azrael clapped his hand over his mouth.

"*It's going to get me, too. Because my bottle is open, and the moment I disappear, you'll forget I exist.*"

He crouched over, breathing hard.

"*Now listen to me: you are being played, master-of-mine. Someone is using memory magic on you. But nobody yet won a game of memory magic with Azrael of the Shroud. You are going to beat this thing. I have complete faith in you, dear boy.*"

"Lucy!" bellowed Azrael. "Lucy, I'm here!" He started running along the beach, calling as he went. *Gods damn it, how big is this island?* Azrael stopped moving. *It's not an island. It's a dream space. The coast looks a little like the Shrouded Isle. The hedge maze, too. That means the details have been filled in by me. Or someone else who lives with me. Lucy, maybe. Or… Or…*

Azrael clenched his fists. He remembered the book, the gate he was building in his garden. *It's all a trap.*

His thoughts were interrupted as something answered his call—not a voice, but a kind of bark. Azrael heard splashing in the rolling fog. He had no idea what to expect, but he took a chance and called out anyway, "Over here! Lucy?"

An animal paddled into view. It was not a dragon. As it reached shallower water, Azrael saw that it was an enormous red-gold wolf. The creature bounded out of the surf and ran towards him. "Lord Azrael!"

Azrael was profoundly confused. "Tod?"

Tod stopped in front of him, dripping and panting. "Lord Azrael," he gasped. "Are you…are you in your right mind?"

"I'm not sure," said Azrael cautiously. "I'm clearly being practiced upon with memory magic. You're not a demon. How did you end up here?"

"I came looking for Jessica," said Tod. "She's been missing for days, and you don't seem to remember her or Mal."

Azrael's chest constricted. It was difficult to breathe. "What did you say?"

Tod's golden eyes scanned his face. "Jessica. Mal." His voice sounded pleading. "They're your demons, your…lovers."

Azrael licked his lips. "That's impossible." He felt sick. It was as though his body was responding with emotions in spite of the fact that he had no connected memories.

Tod's tail drooped. "You don't remember them."

"I…" Azrael passed a hand over his face. *Focus on what you know.* "I remember Lucy. I have an anchor to her—this coat. She doesn't have an anchor to me, though, so it's not perfect. I remember her, but I'm still missing pieces of myself." He hugged the coat around him, drumming his fingers against his shoulder, thinking furiously. "Tell me about this demon you came looking for."

Tod licked his lips. "She's in another…dream, I think. It's a burned out circus. There's a sorcerer who is trying to hurt her.

She's in the shape of a fox. She never had an animal shape before. She doesn't remember who she is."

Azrael scowled with concentration. "She's an earth-born demon?"

"Yes."

"And she's… Wait, did you say she's my lover?"

The wolf looked uncomfortable. "Yes."

Azrael's confidence in his grasp of the situation felt suddenly tenuous. "I am quite certain I am not in bed with a woman."

"I am quite certain you are," snapped Tod. He raised his head and they glared at each other.

What a conversation to have with my ward. Azrael cleared his throat. "Have you purged your inhibitor charm?"

Tod's flash of defiance vanished, and he turned his head to the side in a placating gesture. "I didn't know how else to find her. You are acting like a madman." An instant later, he thought to add, "In the real world, I mean. My lord."

Azrael screwed up his face. "Alright. First things first. Did you recognize this other sorcerer?"

Tod shook his head. "A young man, looks like he might be from the desert states, nobody I've ever seen before."

Azrael waved a hand. "He's dream-walking. He could have altered his appearance. I need to meet this Jessica person. If I see her and take some of her magic, it will probably trigger my memories of her—perhaps *all* of my memories if we really were…uh, as you say, intimate. It won't work if she's lost her mind, though. A creature of pure magic, running around in the dreamlands… She can't do that for long or she won't have any 'self' to return to."

Tod flinched. "Anything," he said hoarsely. "I'll do anything. Just tell me what."

Azrael looked at him narrowly. "Who is Jessica to you?"

Tod stared at him as though he were asking a supremely complicated question. "She's my friend," said Tod at last. "She's also a succubus. She has to…feed."

Azrael opened his mouth. Shut it again. *You and I are in a stranger relationship than I realized.* His curiosity nearly overcame him. "And you say that I'm…?"

"It's Mal," said Tod desperately. "Mal is the piece you're missing. He's your astral incubus. You've had him since forever. You freed him. I'm pretty sure you've been in love with him as long as I've known you. Do you really not remember?"

Azrael stared at Tod—his assumptions, his self-image, his identity all shifting. *I escaped alone from Polois. I have been alone all my life. That is true. That is a foundational truth.*

Except it isn't. Because I didn't. There was someone else. There has always been someone else.

His mouth felt dry. "I…I need to find these people. Either one of us could wake up at any moment. I need you to break into my rooms."

Tod blinked. "What?"

"There's a secret passage in the back of the library. It leads up to my bedroom. I wouldn't normally send a mortal through the deep stacks. They're full of pocket worlds. But as an uninhibited werewolf, you should be alright. Just don't get distracted by any of the people from the pockets. Find the back wall. There's a false book that you can pull out to open the secret passage. The book is called 'Summoning Trouble.' It's not marked in any way, but it's got a fade-out charm, which makes ordinary people overlook it. Ironically, the scent of the magic should lead *you* right to it."

Tod was looking bewildered. "You want me to break into your rooms, my lord?"

"Yes, I want you to be stealthy about it. I need you to bring me back here, probably by force. I suspect I will resist." He raised one eyebrow at Tod's expression. "You did just say, 'I'll do anything.'"

"Yes, but…break into your bedroom? And…and kidnap you?"

Azrael rolled his eyes. "You've just informed me that you know more than anyone ought to know about my sleeping arrangements. I assume nothing will surprise you."

If wolves could have blushed, Azrael was certain Tod would be glowing. *Sorry, kid. There's no time to be precious about this.* "You need to be ready before I wake up. There is no time to lose if you want to save your friend. Stop looking at me like that. You're an uninhibited werewolf, Loudain." Azrael spread his hands. He was a slender, fit man, but he knew perfectly well he was not physically intimidating. "You can wrestle me to the ground, I promise."

31

Lucy

"I fell in love when I was thirty-four. He was a charming sorcerer and small-time criminal named Tristan. I had my own business by then, my little empire, my independence. I gave it all to him. I let him bind me. We had some adventures. He became apprenticed to a more formidable sorcerer. Tristan wanted to put me in a vessel. He said it would make me more powerful, allow me to live longer, stay at his side. I had my reservations, but I tucked them away. I let him do it. And he banished me."

Mal raised his head from Lucy's lap. "He did *what?*"

"Sent me to the astral plane," murmured Lucy. She stared out at the whispering sea under the rolling fog.

Mal had gone rigid with what seemed like indignation. "He sent an earth-born demon to the astral plane? Without warning, without instructions? Did he have a way to get you back?"

Lucy shook her head. "He had a collar on me—a collar like yours. I followed the trail like breadcrumbs. I remember being confused and terrified. I remember that something was hunting me—my entity, I imagine. I remember thinking I would never find my way home. That place was so vast, but it wasn't like a forest or a desert or an ocean or…"

"Mortals have no words for the astral plane," said Mal. He'd risen to a sitting position, now on eye level with her. "You came back?"

Lucy nodded. "I came back, but I didn't have a body at first. I was simply bound to the collar. He fashioned it into my perfume bottle, worked some more magic to concentrate my essence inside. He decanted me, and that was the first time I was a dragon."

Mal shook his head. "It seems like so many things could have gone wrong."

Lucy nodded. "I'm sure that, from his point of view, it was an amazingly successful experiment. If he'd lost me...well, he would have had to do something different. He was a risk-taker, my Tristan. As it was, he took me to his mentor and presented me as a sort of final exam. Ultimately, he used my magic to outmaneuver his mentor and kill him some years later."

"Your lover was a monster," said Mal.

"I know." Lucy focused on the waves. "It is pleasant to be in love. People yearn to be in love before they've even met a suitable candidate. Your life makes sense when you are in love. You feel as though you belong.

"When mortals fall *out* of love, they do it slowly, often over years. It is hard to fall out of love all at once—to go from blind, passionate devotion to clear, unflinching insight. But the astral plane burned away my humanity. At least that's how it seemed to me.

"I looked upon my lover with dragon eyes, and I saw him for exactly what he was—a superficially charming man with a handsome face and a clever wit, but not an ounce of compassion or empathy. I looked back over our time together and realized that every decision he'd made had been for his own advancement. I'd made sacrifices for him; he'd never made one for me. Indeed, he had nearly sacrificed my life, mostly out of curiosity."

"He was a monster," repeated Mal.

"You remind me of him." Lucy spoke without malice, but she also made no effort to soften her words. *You want honesty? There you go.*

Mal didn't say anything. He was still and quiet for so long that Lucy finally turned to look at him. Mal had transformed back into a man. He was hugging his knees to his chin, staring into the fire. His eyes looked wet.

Lucy sighed. "But not always. Not entirely. Come on, Mal, be a cat again." *I know you need to be touched. You practically crawled into my lap the moment you saw me.*

But Mal did not transform into a cat. He cleared his throat. "How long had you been in your bottle when we found you, Lucy?"

Lucy considered. "About eighty years, I think. My previous master made an ill-fated attempt to take the Shrouded Isle from the lake spirit. He died and dropped me there in the ruins."

"Eighty years…" whispered Mal. "In a spirit vessel."

Lucy shrugged. "It's not the longest my bottle has ever been lost. I was in there for almost a hundred and fifty years at one point. I'd go to sleep and wake up and go to sleep again. I tried to figure out how to die once, but I don't think I can from inside my bottle."

Mal scrubbed a hand across his face. "I never asked, did I?"

"Never asked what?"

"How long you'd been in there."

Lucy looked at him quizzically. "I'm sure you didn't. Azrael did, of course. Do you even remember coming to the Shrouded Isle, Mal? You were still pretty...wild."

"It's like a dream," admitted Mal. "Fragments. I do remember finding your bottle. You were so cranky..."

Lucy snorted a laugh. "I was decanted after eighty years by an earnest but naïve teenaged sorcerer with more talent than skill, no training, and an astral incubus, with whom he was hopelessly in love. I gave Azrael about a month before he died and lost my bottle again."

Mal choked on a laugh. "Lucy, I'm sorry."

Lucy shrugged. "About Tristan? I got him killed a few years later—made him overreach himself in a battle, watched while his enemy's spider golem tore him to pieces. Avarice can be just as deadly as any other vice. He didn't think I was capable of—"

"No," interrupted Mal, "I'm *sorry*. For me. For everything." His eyes looked unnaturally bright, his face little more than shadows.

Lucy noticed with alarm that bits of his hair seemed to be streaming into the wind. "Mal...why don't you be a cat again."

He gave a watery smile. "I'm not sure I can. I didn't mean to shift just now. I'm having trouble holding my shape." He held up a hand and they both watched as it disintegrated into whirling black smoke. Mal shut his eyes, made an obvious effort, and pulled his essence back to reform his hand. It was thoroughly transparent in the firelight.

Mal spoke in a rush. "You might as well eat me, Lucy. Otherwise, the dreamcatcher will. Maybe then you'll have enough strength to survive until someone cracks this thing open. Tell Azrael and Jessica I love them. Even if you don't think I can love anyone, tell them I said so."

Lucy was silent for a long moment. "Come here, dove."

Mal scooted against her. He was trembling.

Lucy put an arm around him. She sat up straight and turned his face towards hers with a finger. Mal swallowed. She tucked a strand of dark curls behind his ear.

His face crumpled. "Lucy, this is the opposite of quick. I know I'm not supposed to be scared, but I am *so* scared. Please…"

"Mal," she said patiently, "I told you: you are not going to die. I am not going to let you." Then she kissed him.

32

Mal

Mal was not often surprised by kisses. He was shocked by this one. Lucy's magic hit him like water on parched ground, and he soaked it up without meaning to—a drowning man grasping at a fellow swimmer. An instant later, he pulled away, struggling to regain control of himself. He had Lucy's face in both hands.

She ran her tongue over her lip. "Gods below, Mal. Did you just bite me?"

"S-sorry. Did you just kiss me?"

"Yes, of course I kissed you. How else am I supposed to get magic into you?"

Mal stared at her. "But…the dreamcatcher will eat you, too! I know you said there's a piece of you in your bottle, but without a way to feed, you'll be drained eventually."

Lucy gave him a dragon smile with too many teeth. "My bottle isn't just void, Mal. It's *the* void. A little piece of the astral plane. Haven't you ever wondered why I don't have to feed as long as I can sleep there for a while?"

Mal gaped at her. "That's why you're almost as strong as an astral demon," he whispered.

"Azrael can't figure out how it was done," continued Lucy. "Some lost technique, probably forbidden since the Rift Wars."

Mal swallowed. "So…the dreamcatcher really can't eat you up?"

Lucy shrugged. "I don't think so. I guess we'll find out. I do have every confidence that Azrael will crush this thing. Unfortunately, it doesn't look like he'll manage to do that before it digests you. I will not let that happen."

Mal's vision was coming and going. "Thank you?" *Am I really not about to die?* He'd been so braced for it. He realized that he still had his large hands on either side of Lucy's deceptively delicate face, her fine, silvery hair between his fingers. He didn't know if that was right. He was afraid to say, *Do you actually want me? Because I'm not sure how well this will work otherwise.* Their power differential was so great now that Lucy might as well have been warded for all he could sense of her desires.

"I'm not exactly at my best," whispered Mal.

Lucy rolled her eyes. She kissed him again and didn't stop. Her magic shuddered through Mal like fire on dry leaves, like color in a gray world, like life. Mal's arms slid around her instinctively, one hand spread over her back against the soft fabric of her sweater, the other wrapping around her hip. Mal could feel her spine move under his fingers. He broke the kiss with an effort and rested his forehead against hers, shivering. "Gods, that's good. Lucy, Lucy… Tell me where to put my hands. I don't know—"

"You're fine," said Lucy. She was breathing a little more quickly. Mal wondered if he was taking too much magic. He couldn't tell. His sense of proportion had vanished with his ability to regulate his shape. Lucy slid her arms around his neck. They were still sitting side by side, snuggled together on the sand.

Mal kissed her forehead. He had to force himself not to lick her like a lollipop. Lucy tilted her face up, and her deep blue eyes flashed gold. She had color in her cheeks. Her parted lips looked red with more than lipstick. Mal felt a strange sense of having stumbled into something beyond him. She was classy, sophisticated, mysterious, expensive. She was far too refined for him, but he *wanted* her.

Mal blinked and then giggled like a boy. "You are using magic on me."

Lucy laughed, too. Mal tucked his head against her shoulder, shivering and kissed the side of her neck above her sweater. "It's working."

"Of course it's working. I am Avarice."

"How desperate do you want me? I'm already so hungry it hurts."

Lucy snickered against his ear. "Avarice and Lust are actually quite similar. They're both about desire." She ran her tongue around the rim of his ear, and Mal couldn't repress a whimper. "But your magic is all about sex, and mine has more scope."

"You win?"

Lucy sighed. "I do feel rather as though I'm taking advantage. You seem like a puppy to me. You, Azrael, Jessica—puppies, the lot of you."

Mal pulled back to give her a raised eyebrow. "I am older than you, Lucy. I am technically ageless." He leaned closer and murmured. "Azrael likes the human side of me, but if you want the astral incubus older than stars…I can be that, too."

"Is the older-than-stars version less whiny?" whispered Lucy with mock sincerity. "I had no idea such a version of you existed!"

"Fuck you," said Mal sweetly.

Lucy kissed him again.

33

Azrael

Azrael woke, sitting up in his bed. He was not surprised to find a pen in his hand. The words on his headboard had become deep grooves: "Something is feeding on"

There followed the beginning of a letter that seemed to waver and die. He'd traced the previous letters over and over, but he couldn't seem to finish the sentence.

I must have a moment of lucidity when I wake. Then I lose it.

He saw that he was wearing his nightshirt. However, overtop of it, he was also wearing the fur coat. *I'm supposed to keep it on. Was that my idea? Or the script's?*

Azrael got out of bed, feeling stiff and unwell, and walked across the room to his wardrobe. The project in his garden was almost finished, and the guests would be arriving tomorrow. He needed to install the finishing touches. He needed—

Something shot out from under his bed. Azrael caught a glimpse of it in the mirrored door of his wardrobe—a naked man, preternaturally fast. *Assassin!* Azrael's hand dove for the pocket of the fur cape.

"I'm afraid I can't let you do that, my lord." The man clamped Azrael's arms behind his back in a grip like iron. To his horror, Azrael felt the cold touch of spelled steel on his wrists—instruments that he'd created years ago for dealing with magical creatures. A pair had been in the bottom drawer of his wardrobe, forgotten. *How did he know?*

In desperation, Azrael reached for magic to blast this villain into the Shadow Lands and beyond. However, his power seemed strangely blunted. The spell that hissed out between his teeth barely made this attacker grunt.

Azrael caught a flash in the mirror—silver around the other man's neck. *My focus!* Why hadn't he worn it to bed? Why had he ever taken it off?

Azrael finally got a good look at his attacker's face. "You backstabbing little shit!" he snarled. "You ungrateful cur! Did your family put you up to this? I should have drowned you on the day you arrived like the unwanted whelp you are! I'll make you sorry they didn't bury you on your home island with a silver stake through your heart. I'll use you as bait for a chimera trap and send whatever's left to your bitch mother!"

Tod Loudain looked pale as milk in the mirror over Azrael's shoulder. "My lord, please, I am so sorry, but you told me to do this."

Azrael attempted to break Tod's nose with a swift lash of his head, but Tod dodged with a speed that suggested he'd jettisoned his inhibitor. Of course he had. He dragged Azrael across the floor, swearing and thrashing. "You're the one who's responsible for this memory magic, aren't you? Thief. You will not get away with this."

"My lord, please! I am trying to help you."

"I'm not going to feed you to chimera after all," panted Azrael as Tod threw him down across his own bed, face planted in a pillow. "I am going to put such a collar on you that demons will weep to see it. You want to be a wolf? I'll make you a wolf for all your days. I'll chain you to my gates to keep watch, never to speak to another soul, and prolong your miserable life with magic until the stars burn out."

Azrael could feel the young man trembling against him. He was leaning heavily on Azrael's back, pinning him to the bed, fumbling for something in a bedside drawer with his free hand. Azrael had thought that Tod was naked simply because he'd come as a wolf, but this position suggested something else. *Does he intend to violate me before killing me?*

Azrael searched frantically for some way to reach his own magic through the haze of the spelled steel without his focus. *Or maybe not without it.* Azrael arched his back, bringing the nape of his neck into contact with the necklace against Tod's chest. *Chew on this, you bastard.* He opened his mouth to unleash something truly unpleasant...and Tod poured a quarter-full shot glass of fluid between his lips.

Azrael coughed, gagged. He started to say the words he'd been preparing, but his tongue felt thick. Tod backed off of him. The necklace broke contact with his skin, and the chance was lost. Azrael spun around, still cuffed, sliding off the bed to sit on the floor. He glared at Tod through the drugged haze. The young man stood there naked, trembling and hugging himself. "Lord Azrael, please don't be angry. I am so sorry. I'm doing what you asked."

"Fuck you," slurred Azrael and fell asleep.

34

Mal

Mal was growing more solid. He hadn't stopped to look, but he could feel his own essence coalescing, his control of his shape improving, the full range of his senses returning. He got a better grip on the magical transference between himself and Lucy and slowed it down. Feeding on her was like eating something rich with more cream than sugar—easy to go too fast. He still had no idea what she wanted sexually or how much magic she could truly afford to give him. She was cloaking expertly. As usual. Mal had pushed through Lucy's cloaking in the past with brute force, but he wasn't about to try that now.

Mal broke off kissing at last and moved a hand from behind Lucy's back to look at it. His skin shone like warm caramel in the firelight. It had pores, tiny hairs, it looked like skin, not smoke! Lucy made a little noise of satisfaction. Mal let out a long breath. His eyes skipped over the fire—burning not just orange, but blue and green with sea salt. The blue-gray waves seemed a little louder. Even the mist overhead looked brighter, with shades of pearl and blue-black. "The world has colors again," he breathed.

Lucy's warm tongue met his throat, making him exhale sharply. Her teeth nibbled his skin—sharper than human teeth ought to be. Mal shut his eyes and swallowed. As he drew away from the edge of disintegration, his more basic instincts were asserting themselves. He was uncomfortably aware of his cock, rigid against his leg.

"Lucy, what do you want me to do? You can give me magic this way. Obviously. We don't have to do anything else. But it would help me know how to respond if you'd tell me what you want."

Lucy backed off a fraction. "Gods, Mal, that almost sounded like good and considerate communication."

He gave a shaky grin. "I communicate *really* well…in certain situations."

Lucy's dark blue eyes were practically glowing. "Stop right here, hmm? Do you want to?"

"Of course I don't want to!"

"It does sound anticlimactic."

Mal's arousal and curiosity flared. *Maybe she does want more.* Mal leaned close to her ear. "Can I put my hands where I want, Lucy?"

"Try it, and we'll find out."

Mal laughed. "I can't decide whether that's an invitation or a threat."

Lucy laughed with him. "You want me to stop cloaking, don't you?"

"Desperately."

"Too bad."

"Lucy!"

Mal trailed a knuckle over her face, past the edge of her jaw, along the pulse of her throat, over her collarbone, across the soft fabric of her sweater, over a breast. He paused to circle the nipple with a thumb. She was wearing a brassiere, but the material wasn't thick.

Mal kept his eyes on Lucy's, and she stared back, her expression unreadable. She swallowed at last as he ran his thumb in circles. Mal drew a delicate line along the edge of her brassiere above the sweater. "Can you get rid of this?"

"That would make me feel like I'm wearing pajamas," said Lucy, her voice a little huskier than before.

"*I* am wearing my pajamas," Mal pointed out.

"Fair."

He ran his knuckles down her stomach, past the edge of the sweater. He paused here, watching her face, and then pushed his hand up under the sweater against her bare skin. He felt her breathing speed up a fraction, saw her pupils dilate. Mal moved his hand back up, and when he reached her breast, it was bare. He cupped the curve of warm flesh, ran his thumb back and forth over the nipple, feeling it harden.

Lucy's ribcage was very definitely rising and falling faster against his chest. She was blinking. Mal finally kissed her, and she made a low noise into his mouth. Her tongue slid against his, one of her hands tangling in his hair. Mal ran kisses from her mouth down the side of her throat. "You are so pretty, Lucy."

"We've established that I'm an old lady," she said and then caught her breath as Mal cupped her other breast.

"And I'm older than stars. And you're really pretty."

She also felt fragile. Mal knew that was deceptive. Lucy was a dragon, and she could still eat him. But her relaxed skin made her bones feel like delicate sculpture under warm satin.

Mal ran his fingers down her bare spine, feeling the ridges and shifting muscles. He wanted to run his hands over her hips, but he didn't dare.

Mal had fed mostly on younger people during his life on the Shrouded Isle. This wasn't because he had any preference. He could feed on people of any age who had clear sexual desires. Unlike a human man, he had no instinct that guided him towards women in their childbearing years. However, the Shrouded Isle took mostly young courtiers because Azrael thought this was least disruptive. By the time a person was in their early twenties, their sexual preferences were clear enough for Mal to feed easily. However, their lives hadn't really started yet. Azrael took volunteers who were unmarried and had no dependents. Political guests were usually older, but Mal rarely fed directly on them. He had experienced a few liaisons with older people during his months abroad, but no one remotely like Lucy.

"You're a fine one to talk about pretty," she said. "Those eyelashes are ridiculous." Her tone was affectionate, her fingers light on his face. Mal turned his head to catch one finger in his mouth. He grasped it gently in his teeth, rubbed his tongue over the tip. He kissed his way between her fingers, exploring the sensitive skin.

He looked up at her through his lashes, and Lucy's eyes flashed gold. Mal let go of her finger to say, "How do you do that? I can't do that!"

Lucy didn't answer. She pushed against him. Mal realized that he had been leaning into her with the vague notion of laying her down on her back and covering her with kisses. There was an awkward moment as they both tried to reposition, lost their balance, and collapsed sideways onto the sand.

Mal barked a laugh. "We're both tops, aren't we? Has that always been the problem?"

"Did you *just* figure that out?"

"This is your show, Lucy-Lu. You're saving my life. You do whatever you want."

"Well, then, I want to get rid of your pajamas."

Mal did that. Lucy pushed him onto his back and climbed on top. She straddled his belly, just a little higher than Mal would have liked, and made her sweater disappear in a shower of golden dust that briefly covered them and then vanished. She was still wearing her full, dark blue skirt. It felt like wool. But if she'd been wearing any underwear, she'd already gotten rid of it. Mal could feel her soft wetness pressing against his stomach.

"Lucy, Lucy..." He reached up to stroke her breasts. "Can I kiss you here?"

"Gods, yes."

Lucy started to lean over him. Mal reached down to her hips and dragged her up his body. He sat up, cradling her, and caught a nipple in his mouth. Mal felt intensely satisfied by her groan of pleasure, the way her legs clenched around his torso, her hands in his hair. He was frankly amazed at her self-control. In spite of the fact that he couldn't see her desires, Mal was well-acquainted with the effects of his own feeding. He'd taken quite a bit of magic from Lucy. *How is she not flat on her back underneath me?*

Mal lavished kisses on her breasts, enjoying every gasp and squirm. It would have been easier if he'd just flipped her over in the sand, but if that made her feel too helpless, well…he could work with this.

Mal slid a hand under her ass to pull her up higher and more tightly against his him. Lucy responded by wrapping her legs more snugly around his body. Mal pulled his hand back and ran it slowly up her bare leg. When Lucy didn't protest, he moved it all the way to her bare ass under her dress.

Mal took a moment to savor that situation and then pressed his hand further underneath. She was *so* wet. And she wasn't saying no. Mal slid two fingers into her slippery warmth, and her muscles fluttered around him. *You are right on the edge.*

He raised his head from her breasts, and they were nose-to-nose. Lucy had a flush of pink across her cheek bones. Her lips looked too-kissed. Mal moved his fingers, and her eyes snapped shut. Her lips parted. The muscles of her belly and thighs tensed.

Mal kissed her on the nose, and she opened her eyes again. "Lucy, you're *really* good at cloaking…but I'm an incubus…and you've given me a *lot* of magic."

Mal moved his fingers, searching for the sweet spot. Lucy's pelvic muscles fluttered again. Her eyes narrowed to slits. Her breathing accelerated through her parted lips. "That comes with a few unavoidable side effects," continued Mal. He found the right spot, the right angle, and rubbed hard.

Lucy made a guttural noise, her hands fisting in his hair. Mal could sense her holding herself back by force of will. "Gods,

Lucy, anyone else would be begging me for it by now. Please just let me get you off—"

Lucy pulled his mouth to hers and kissed him savagely. Her pussy clamped so hard around Mal's fingers that he made a noise of surprise against her mouth.

Mal kissed her until she relaxed. When she pulled away, he said, "Can I get you naked yet? Have I earned that?"

Lucy let out a long sigh. She sat up, still straddling Mal's lap, and he lay back in the sand. Lucy made her skirt disappear with a rustle of gold. She sat there looking down at him. Mal ran his hands along her legs and sides, enjoying the feel of her hip bones. He brushed a thumb through the silver and steel curls between her legs.

Lucy was letting herself look at him, too. Mal could feel her eyes tracing the contours of his arms and chest. "Can you believe we're doing this?" she whispered.

Mal grinned. "We're dreaming. Sort of."

"You have never figured in my dreams quite this way before."

That felt like an invitation to squabble, but Mal ignored it. "You came back from the astral plane. I don't know anyone else who's done that. Ren and Jessica have no idea what it's like. I wish I'd known. I could have talked to you about it."

Lucy's expression softened. "You still can."

"If we survive."

"We'll survive." Lucy's lips twisted up at the edges. "You were speaking of self-control…" She backed down his body until her ass brushed his erection.

Mal swallowed convulsively. "You don't have to do anything about that if you don't want to."

Lucy looked at him narrowly. "You are not what I expected in bed, Mal."

"Too slow?"

"No." She traced the muscles of his belly in a way that made his balls tighten. "A sweetheart."

Mal felt strangely warm. He started to say something and then Lucy grinned. "So I am going to torture you a bit more."

"How's that?"

She sat up straight, bumping his cock again. "I'm going to teach you to cloak."

35

Azrael

Azrael opened his eyes. He was sitting on the sand. His focus was around his neck. He clutched at it frantically, drew on his own magic to reassure himself.

He was not reassured. His magic felt strange—oily, contaminated. Azrael jerked his hand away. "Tod!" He thrust his hands into the pockets of the cape, hoping Tod had really followed all of his instructions.

But none of it will do any good if he couldn't follow me. "Tod!"

The wolf slunk out of the mist. He looked at Azrael cautiously from a few paces away.

Azrael shut his eyes and took a deep breath. "It's alright. I'm... I remember telling you to do that." Azrael grimaced as the details of the scene in the bedroom returned to him. He remembered exactly what he'd thought and said. Weirdly, he also remembered standing on this beach and telling Tod to do it.

Azrael stifled his mounting impatience to get this situation under control. He crouched down to look at the wolf levelly. "Thank you. I hope I didn't hurt you."

"I'm a werewolf," said Tod in a voice that sounded far from wolfish. "I'm hard to hurt."

I don't think that's actually true. "Tod, please come here."

He came hesitantly. *He's not that big.* A strange thought, since the wolf stood to his waist. Azrael had a vague idea that he'd seen a bigger animal, though, recently. A bigger tame animal? *Lucy?* It seemed like something else.

Tod did not meet his eyes. "Sir, I am well aware of what you could do to me. And I know spitting out my inhibitor broke your rules…"

Azrael put a hand on the wolf's shoulder. "When you came to the Shrouded Isle, you were only seven. But you were so solemn, so well-behaved. You didn't need another parent. You had two perfectly good ones and a clan of other relatives besides. That's just as well, because I would have made a terrible parent."

The wolf gave a cough that sounded like a laugh.

"What I said just now in the bedroom..." Azrael wanted to say, *I would never do any of those things to you.* But, obviously, under the right circumstances, he would. Tod was no fool. The Azrael he'd just wrestled to the ground and drugged was under a delusion, but he wasn't actually another person. "I'm afraid you've just seen me at my worst."

Tod raised his eyes to meet Azrael's. He gave the ghost of a smile. "Fortunately, sir, I have also seen you at your best."

Azrael tried to smile back. "I *will* make sure those things don't happen to you. I'll tell you how to kill me if necessary."

"Oh, sir." Tod put his head on Azrael's shoulder in a doggy hug. "It won't come to that. You'll figure this out."

Azrael took a deep breath. "Your grandfather is arriving with the early group. I think I'm going to kill him if I'm not restored to my senses."

Tod flinched. "I wondered about that." He pulled away. "But you'll figure it out before then. Trust me, as soon as you remember Mal, you'll be ready to rip the world apart to set this right."

"I feel ready to rip the world apart as it is!" Azrael stood up. "Let's go find your friend."

36

Mal

Mal groaned. "I've tried to learn before, Lucy. I know I'm supposed to hold onto emotions that are the opposite of my nature. I can sort of do it for a few seconds, but it doesn't last. I don't understand how you manage to do it for hours."

Lucy shook her head. "The textbooks don't describe this well. Nobody really wants demons to cloak. Magicians don't want demons who are even better at deception, and demons aren't often anxious to help each other."

Mal grimaced.

"I can't tell you if my way is the best," continued Lucy. "It's just what I learned through trial and error. Here's the secret: cloaking is like striking a bell. Once struck, the vibrations continue for a while. You don't have to ring the bell constantly. You just have to renew it now and then."

Mal leaned up on his elbows, keenly interested. "So what's the bell?"

"That's what you have to figure out for yourself. It's usually an idea that sparks an emotion that runs cross-grain to your essential nature. You have to be a little bit human to cloak."

And you think I am. Mal remembered something she'd said to him at a wedding in the Provinces weeks ago. "Are we Love and Generosity, Lucy?"

She tried to repress a smile. "Well, I certainly feel that I'm being quite generous, although you won't think so in a moment. Learning to cloak is like finding the perfect musical note to shatter a piece of glass. You can't really find it or test it without something in your own nature to push against. It's a quality in opposition, you see?"

Mal frowned. "Not really."

"I had to learn in jewelry stores," said Lucy. "Beautiful places, swimming in avarice. You, on the other hand…" She lifted her body a little, backed up over Mal's softening cock, and settled down with her warm crotch on top of his length, pressing against his lower belly.

Instantly, Mal's flagging arousal soared. He let out his breath in a hiss. Lucy ran her body up and down his shaft a few times, getting him wet. Mal settled his hands on her hips, resisting the urge to slide her onto his cock like a delightful glove. Lucy paused, the head of his dick pressed against her entrance, and looked at him…then through him, at his aura.

Mal looked back at her, breathing fast.

"Well, you're certainly radiating lust," said Lucy. "You say you love Azrael and Jessica. Show me."

37

Jessica

Jessica stood by the circus wall for what felt like a long time, waiting for the wolf to return. She liked the wolf. His scent reminded her of safety and warmth and contentment. And, of course, he had rescued her from the terrifying man in the cellar.

Jessica was a patient creature, but she did not like the rolling mist beyond the wall. It reminded her of being lost in a breathless void, helplessly drifting without sight or sound or smells. Jessica remained by the wall for as long as she could tolerate it, but after a while, her proximity to the formless emptiness became unbearable. So she made her way back to the circus gates and went inside.

She wandered for a while, careful to avoid the lane with the cellar. At last, she came upon a large, echoing building with a hole in the roof. The place was dim inside, but Jessica didn't find it frightening. There was a platform and rows of velvet-padded seats, now decaying. Jessica had a vague memory of sitting in seats like this before. Something had happened on the platform, something exciting. There had been noises and lights and other people.

Jessica hopped up onto one of the seats. She was a patient creature. She would wait. Maybe something would happen.

Jessica might have sat there forever, patiently watching the empty platform, but at last she heard a noise in the back of the room and turned to see the wolf trotting up the aisle. Someone else walked behind him. "Jessica!" exclaimed the wolf. "Gods below, I wish you had stayed by the wall!"

He reached her seat, and she licked his muzzle. He sighed and looked up at the other person, who'd stopped beside her chair. This person smelled a little like the frightening man in the cellar. But, underneath, Jessica caught a tantalizing hint of something else. She leaned forward, sniffing. He was like a creature who had rolled in filth, but underneath, he smelled like… "Home."

Jessica snapped her jaws shut in surprise. She had not known she could do that. She looked desperately from the wolf to the new man. "Home?"

The man and the wolf were talking. Jessica couldn't follow what they said. She hopped up on the arm of the chair to get closer to the man's fascinating scent. He turned towards her and put both hands gently on her body. Jessica's world went white.

38

Azrael

Azrael was as surprised as anyone else when a jolt of magic leapt between his hands and the fox. He had expected some difficulty in getting at Jessica's magic. He couldn't remember her full name and Tod didn't know it, either. So he couldn't bind her. He'd anticipated something mildly complicated, such as taking some of her fur and working a limited binding. He certainly hadn't expected the white light that leapt between them or the alarming phenomena of his fingers sinking for an instant *into* the fox.

Azrael had one baffled moment to think, *But that would only make sense if she already had my magic in her.* Then his world cracked like an eggshell. Azrael's own pure, untainted magic poured back into him and he *remembered*.

In the same instant, Jessica changed. Her red and white fur ran together in a curl of smoke, and she was a woman— naked, her blond hair tangled and wild, her blue eyes as round as marbles. Jessica clapped a hand to her mouth. "Oh, gods!"

Azrael staggered backwards. "Fuck, fuck, fuck, fuck…!" He gripped the row of seats behind him. "How could I have let this happen? Mal… Shit, shit, shit. Jessica, say something."

"Where am I?" She was patting herself down as though to be sure of her body. Making clothes took skill and magic to spare, and Azrael doubted she had either at the moment.

"Do you know who I am?" he asked.

"Lord Azrael?" she said in a small voice.

Azrael swallowed. *Please say I haven't come too late.* "Anyone else?"

Jessica sniffled. "Ren?"

Azrael opened his arms in a gesture that still seemed alien to him, and she folded against his chest. Then they were both crying.

39

Mal

"Lucy, I can't. I just can't. I'm not good at this." Mal was practically weeping with frustration. He'd been trying to cloak for what felt like hours in the hellish time-dilation of the dream space. He'd forced himself to relive numerous tender moments in spite of the distraction of Lucy's teasing. Mal examined his pride in the things Azrael could do with Mal's magic, the intimacy of that connection, the comfort Mal took in their familiar patterns together. He relived holding hands for the first time, kissing, making love, eating breakfast together, even arguing when they could complete each other's sentences.

Mal recalled the first time Jessica had come looking for him—the thrill of finding someone like himself, the pleasure in talking about his nature to someone who understood it. He recalled the way her magic filled him a sense of wonder that he'd thought only humans could experience, the way she'd always seen him as a person with choices, had always believed that

Mal's future was not a foregone conclusion. "She said I could have a happy ending. Nobody ever thought that before. Even Azrael just thought we were going to die together."

Mal tried telling Lucy some of these things. The stories made him blush more than he'd expected, considering they mostly weren't about sex. He tried thinking his way through them. He reached for those feelings, the particular flavor of those moments. Whenever he started to get too deep in his recollections, Lucy would grind against him, bringing a flood of his most natural instincts. She would look at his aura and shake her head. "That's not it."

Mal put both hands over his face. He was slick with sweat. His balls ached. "Maybe I'm not human enough. Maybe I just can't."

40

Jessica

Jessica sat beside Azrael in the dream of a burned out theater, wearing Lucy's cape and a piece of charred stage curtain they'd found on the floor. Azrael appeared to be wearing one of his suits. "Probably because it's how I think of myself," he tried to explain. "I'm just a mortal dreaming, while you're currently a creature of pure magic inhabiting the dreamlands."

Tod had gone to stand watch at the door after Jessica covered his nose in kisses and told him what a handsome wolf he made. "I knew I needed to talk to her," Azrael told him, "but I need to say more than I thought. Give us a moment."

However, they didn't say anything for a few long seconds after Tod's departure. Jessica understood now what she was seeing. The rest of the curtain hung in tatters high above them. Props lay strew and broken in the shadows beyond. "I was thinking of the play in Tanisea," she said at last, "the one where Mal held your hand. I couldn't remember any of that, though. I just knew this place felt nice—like something wonderful might happen. So I stayed and waited. I think I might have sat here forever, watching that empty stage, waiting for something to happen."

Azrael swallowed. He turned his hand over on the armrest and slid it under Jessica's, lacing their fingers together. "Jessica, I am so sorry. I should have been more careful."

Jessica ran her fingers back and forth through his, feeling the delicate bones and calluses. "Where is Mal?" Her voice only shook a little.

"Trapped in a dream space," said Azrael, "and I think his magic is being siphoned away. He thinks…" Azrael's voice caught. "He thinks it's a spirit vessel. He thinks I put him there. I saw him in a dream, but I didn't know who he was."

Jessica squeezed his fingers. "He'll understand once you explain."

"Being alone is so hard for him. But," Azrael gave an uneasy laugh, "I suppose he's not alone now, because Lucy went after him. Gods, I hope she didn't eat him. Surely she cares enough about me not to eat him."

Jessica's eyebrows rose. "Mal and Lucy are trapped together in a dream space? With nobody else?"

"Looks that way."

They'll either fuck or kill each other. Possibly both. Jessica decided not to share her conclusions.

Azrael was staring at her hand with a look of fierce concentration. "Mal said something to me the day before all this started. In my tower after…after he turned me over my desk. He said, 'You like demons. We're your best friends.' Then he tried to tell me something about you that he couldn't quite bring himself to say, and I pretended not to understand. But I did. I do. I know what he wanted to ask."

Jessica's throat felt suddenly dry. Her heart thumped painfully against her ribs. She was afraid of what he might say next, so afraid that she would have paused the whole world if she'd had the power. Just to steady herself for a moment, just to get her breath. But Jessica couldn't freeze time.

"I know you want children," he said softly.

Jessica shut her eyes. "I know you think that's unwise."

"I do," agreed Azrael, still running her fingers through his. "But there are ways to avoid passing your demonic magic to your child. You could, for instance, go to the mundane world, take a lover or a husband there, and live out your days far from the

Shattered Sea. This path is poorly studied, but I'm inclined to believe that it works."

He raised his eyes to hers, saw that they were brimming, and leaned forward to smooth the tears away with the thumb of his free hand. "Jessica, I would make such a terrible father."

"No!" she said fiercely through her tears. "You would make a wonderful father!"

"I think Tod might disagree."

Jessica raised her chin. "If Tod is the product of your upbringing, then you have just proved my point. But he's not, and we both know it."

"I should hope not," muttered Azrael, "as we apparently share a lover. Jessica, look at what almost happened to you because of me! You could have faded away here, staring at this stage, waiting for," he wiped his own eyes, "something to happen. People who want to hurt me come after my intimates. My life is chaos! Can't you see that?"

Jessica tried to force her chin to stop quivering. "Your life is not chaos. You get up and go to work at the same time every day. You wear practically the same suit every day. You have tea at the same time every afternoon. The horses love you because you're so predictable. You say the same things to Mal so often he can quote them in his sleep. Your dressing gown must be as old as I am. You are the most boring man I know!"

They were both laughing and crying at the same time now, and it was hard to breathe. "Except for all the magic," continued Jessica, "and all the adventures in pocket worlds and all the sex. Except for all the beautiful clothes you buy me and all the books you give me and all the funny things you say when you think nobody is listening. Except for that."

Azrael swallowed, clutching her hand. After a moment he said, "Jessica, you came into my life and blew it apart. Mal is the most precious thing in the world to me. You took him—"

"You gave him to me," growled Jessica. "And I know how hard that was, Ren. I know how much you love him and how much you trusted me."

"I gave him to you," agreed Azrael, "and then you gave him back to me." He couldn't find words for a moment. "There is no one I owe a greater debt, Jessica. No one. Sometimes it feels like there's a tremendous power difference between you and me, but I am *very* conscious of how much I owe you. If you leave, it will feel like a limb has been amputated. But I *do* want you to be happy."

"I am happy," said Jessica. She took her courage in both hands and continued, "But I would be happier if, in four or five years, you'd have a baby with me." Jessica held her breath. Now he would say yes or he would say no. Probably no. Jessica felt strangely calm. She would get her answer and make her decision, knowing what she was choosing between.

Slowly, Azrael let go of her hand. He sat up straighter and threaded his fingers together in his lap. When he spoke, his voice was oddly formal. "This isn't how I planned to do this. I was going to choose some beautiful spot in a storybook—perhaps that hot spring spa you were looking at. I intended to have good food and good music and attractive clothes. I certainly intended to have Mal along."

Jessica looked around at the burned out theater, at the drifting mist through the hole in the roof, at her dress made of curtain scraps. "Your plans seem to have been scotched."

Azrael nodded. "Nevertheless…" He slid to one knee beside her chair. He took her hand and looked up at her. His almond-shaped eyes looked very dark in his pale face.

Jessica's breath caught.

"Jessica Charles—whose full name I know, but will not say in such a place—will you marry me?"

Jessica gaped at him.

Azrael's formal tone slipped a little. He spoke more quickly, "Marry *us?* Mal and me, because we come as a set. He would ask you himself if he were here, but he wouldn't really understand what he was asking, what it meant. I do." Azrael gestured with a shaking hand at Lucy's fur cape. "If you check the pocket…"

Jessica slid her hand numbly into the pocket, and came out with two silver rings. She cradled them in her palm. "You really did plan this," she whispered.

"I made them from a link of Mal's collar."

Jessica's eyes shot to his face.

"They could work like the collar," continued Azrael hesitantly, "if that's something you want. You've joked about it before. I don't know how serious you were. They could do a lot of things with a little blood and a lot of magic. But right now, I'm hoping they'll provide an anchor that will keep me in my right mind long enough to stop this sorcerer who is attacking us. Even if you say no, they'll at least work for that."

Jessica opened her mouth, but Azrael hurried on. "Jessica, I will never feel as sexually attracted to a woman as to a man. You can charm it out of me with magic, but I think you know that's not my normal bent. Gods know Mal is more than ready to fill in the gaps, but…I don't want you to feel unappreciated by a man you've married."

Jessica gave a surprised laugh. "I don't feel unappreciated by you."

"I love you. I trust you. I want you in my life." He swallowed. "And, yes, I will have a baby with you if that's…if you really…" He was shaking all over. Jessica slid off the theater seat and knelt beside him. "You probably need some time to think about it—"

She threw her arms around him. "Yes!" She kissed him on the mouth. Kissed him until he didn't taste like tears anymore. "Yes, yes, yes!"

Azrael made a noise that sounded like relief. He struggled to pull them both to their feet. "I love you, too," said Jessica when they were standing face to face, "and I don't think you ever love two people the same way. I don't love you the same way I love Mal. You don't love me the same way you love Mal. That's alright."

She allowed herself a grin so wide it hurt. "And we're going to have a baby!"

"Not right now?" asked Azrael, his voice pleading.

"Gods, no," said Jessica. "In a few years."

"I have so much research to do…in the locked stacks of forbidden libraries."

Jessica snickered. "Only you would say: 'I'm going to be a father. I have so much research to do.'"

"Are you set upon the child being a demon?" asked Azrael. "Because I'm inclined to see if I can prevent that."

"I'm not set upon anything, except the child being mine and yours," said Jessica, "and Mal's if that's possible."

Azrael raised one eyebrow.

Jessica sighed. "Mal thinks that if you have his magic inside you when we make the baby, it might be sort of his, too. Like literally have some of him in it. I told him that seemed like a stretch."

Azrael frowned. "Actually, he might be right if… Wait a moment, you two have already discussed this?"

Jessica shrugged. *Why did you think he was trying to ask you about it?*

Azrael rolled his eyes. "Has he decided on a position to accomplish this? No, don't tell me."

Jessica giggled. "We looove you."

"Speaking of Mal…" Azrael pulled away from her. "I have to go after him. I have to…" He scrubbed a hand across his face. "I probably can't. My magic is too corrupted. I probably have to break this thing from the outside, from the mortal plane. Shit, shit, shit. I hope Lucy is able to help him. At least maybe she told him I didn't put him there. I would hate for him to think it was me."

At that moment, Tod came hurrying down the aisle. "Time to go," he hissed. "The sorcerer's coming."

41

Azrael

Azrael sat in one of the theater seats, his arms spread along the back, and waited. His decision to do this was a bit foolhardy. He had few weapons here in a world that he did not control, with his own magic tainted. However, he was willing to take the risk to make sure Jessica and Tod had time to escape. He also wanted some hints as to the identity of his attacker. *Show yourself, bastard.*

Tup, tup, tup. The footsteps sounded loud in the silent theater. Azrael refused to turn around. The anger that had been burning underneath his confusion and grief rose hot and bright in his chest. *How dare you take my friends?*

Something slammed into him—a binding spell, but it was intended for demons and it passed like a breath momentarily knocked from his body. Azrael refused to show that he'd felt it, but he was grudgingly impressed. The spell was pure blunt force, no finesse, and it must surely require an absurd amount of power because it did not employ the demon's name. However, it probably would work for a short period of time on all but the strongest entities. His antagonist was apparently taking no chances.

"So," said a voice behind him, "you're Azrael of the Shroud." The voice sounded young—like a teenager—but Azrael knew better than to trust this. His opponent's voice and appearance could be altered, although doing so would require additional magic, and Azrael was beginning to wonder exactly how much magic the man could afford to waste.

Aloud, Azrael said, "Yes, and you're late." He snapped out the words like chips off a block of ice.

The other sorcerer gave a surprised huff.

Azrael stood up smoothly and turned around. The other man was about five paces away. He was certainly maintaining the teenaged persona consistently—a lanky kid who'd just hit his growth spurt and wasn't eating enough. He had dark brown hair and skin, pimples, a scruffy beard, shabby trousers and a rumpled shirt. He slouched in front of Azrael with his hands in his pockets, looking mulish. Azrael had to remind himself that this person—yes, *this* one—had just hit him with a binding spell that would have given the lake spirit pause.

"Any dream-walker who goes around kidnapping people should know better than to make such a bloated, sprawling construction. You can't even monitor the whole thing. Sloppy."

The kid looked unimpressed. "You're supposed to be a big deal."

"Well, I'm certainly a man people don't like to cross. What made you think this was a good idea?"

The kid scratched his beard. "You seem pretty lucid. That's interesting. Did you drain that little fox demon that's been running around? I thought a night terror got her, but maybe not. I suppose draining her would bring you back to yourself for a moment."

A reasonable assumption, though happily incorrect. "Who *are* you?" Direct questions were worth a try. Maybe his enemy would engage in a little grandstanding.

The kid gave a twitch of his lips that was not quite a smile. He shoved his hands into his pockets. "I'm nobody."

"On the contrary, you are somebody who has my full attention in all the wrong ways. If you're hoping to hold my mind or my servants hostage, you'll regret it. Nevertheless, I would like to know what you want."

The kid did smile then. "You're pretty good at keeping your temper, Lord Azrael. Better than most magicians. You want to know my terms? Unfortunately for you, there aren't any. I don't care about you at all. I'm after bigger quarry. Sorry. Now we've both got work to do. You've got to finish my gate, and I've got to hold this whole 'bloated' construction together. So, kindly fuck off, my lord."

Bigger quarry? Suddenly everything made more sense. *Well, you're going to find you've chosen the wrong tool for this job.*

Azrael wasn't surprised when the kid pulled his hand from his pocket and blew a puff of choking dust into Azrael's face. The adolescent voice seemed to echo from a distance. "Wake up, my puppet. We won't meet again. As far as you're concerned, we never did."

"You're wrong," whispered Azrael and hoped, desperately, that he was right.

42

Mal

Lucy sighed. "Let's rest for a moment." Almost to herself, she muttered, "Lust is not a patient creature."

No, thought Mal with a flash of irritation, *no one with a cock would be patient in this situation!*

Lucy ran a finger along the curls of dark hair between his naval and groin. Mal was about to tell her that this did not constitute a rest when she murmured, "He told me the other day that he wants to teach you magic. He wanted to know what I thought of that."

Mal was shocked. He remembered Azrael's desk drawer jumping open beneath his fingers. He remembered his own sense of alarm and Azrael's strangely mild reaction. "I'm sure you told him *exactly* what you thought of that."

Lucy didn't answer. She kept brushing her fingers over his stomach. "What do *you* think? You used to read his grimoires whenever you got the chance."

"I wanted to get loose!" exclaimed Mal. "I *am* loose now, so…doing magic is for humans."

Lucy raised her head to give him a speculative look. "You don't mind being Azrael's magical battery?"

"No." Mal spoke in a small voice, aware of how hypocritical he sounded after so many years of complaining.

Lucy sighed. "The thing is, Mal, he can't bear to think of you as a slave, so he thinks of you as a pet. But he doesn't want to be in bed with his pet, either. He wants a partner."

Mal felt bewildered. "Sometimes I like being his pet."

Lucy gave a snort of laughter. "Sometimes he likes petting you."

"You certainly do," said Mal and Lucy rolled her eyes.

"But you are part of the persona he has created for himself," she continued. "He wants to give you a lot more autonomy in that role. Can you handle it?"

Mal swallowed. *I can't even handle cloaking, apparently.* "I don't know, Lucy. I'll try. Teaching magic seems like apprentice stuff. I'm not his apprentice."

All of this talking about Azrael and Jessica had brought back Mal's sense of grief. *Jessica will feel so alone in the void. Then, if she can't escape, she'll slowly come unraveled. I can't imagine a worse way to die. And Azrael... What if he figures out what's happened, but he can't get us back? What if he thinks he killed me... draining magic out of the artifact, bleeding me to death? He'll think I died believing he betrayed me. He'll think about that for the rest of his life.*

Lucy's voice—strangely gentle. "Mal, that's not helping."

Mal didn't bother to respond. He was certain that Lucy could see the grief in his aura, and of course it was the wrong emotion. Everything he did was wrong. He felt so tired.

I wish we were all in bed reading and Azrael and Jessica were talking about which book to visit next. I wish Azrael was picking out dresses for Jessica and he'd let her have that baby, and I could help them do it. I wish I was home.

"Mal." The timbre of Lucy's voice had changed. Mal opened his eyes. She was staring at his aura. "What are you thinking about right now?"

"Jessica and Azrael doing stuff together."

Lucy didn't take her eyes off his aura. "What sort of stuff?"

"Reading, dressing, kissing, I don't know, Lucy. Stuff we do together."

"But without you?"

"Well, not completely…but, I guess…sort of."

Lucy ground her pelvis against him. Mal did not want his body to respond. He wanted to rest. But he was an incubus, and that came with certain unavoidable side effects. Lucy kept gliding up and down his length, and at last he grimaced and clamped his hands on her hips. "Lucy, I think we should be done now."

"Oh, we are."

Mal looked up. Lucy was grinning. "You're cloaking, Mal."

"I— What?"

"Your aura is totally opaque. Your body is responding, but I can't see lust in your aura. The chord you've struck is powerful enough to obliterate the signs of your own essential nature. If it can hide your essential nature, it can hide the rest of your thoughts and feelings. That's cloaking."

Mal tilted his head back, weak with wonder and relief. "Azrael and Jessica together—"

"Prompt unselfish emotions in you, apparently."

"Can I finish now? I'll do it myself; all you have to do is get off me."

Lucy tilted her head. "Is that what you want?"

"You keep asking that question."

"I always wondered whether you actually had desires of your own or whether you simply mirror your partner."

Mal felt indignant. "Of course I have desires of my own!"

"Then what do you want?"

"I want to flip you over and fuck the shit out of you." He was sure Lucy would find this expression vulgar, but right now he didn't care.

Lucy stretched, arching her body like a cat, and then slid his cock inside her. "Alright."

Mal groaned. He almost came right then. He would have if her last word wasn't reverberating in his head. "Did you just say—?"

"Do you really need to be told twi—?"

He flipped her over.

Mal covered Lucy's mouth in a savage kiss, hips driving hard between her legs. She growled, bit his lip, her nails digging into his shoulders and back. She bucked so hard that he might have worried that she didn't actually want it…except that her legs clamped around his waist like a vise. She climaxed an instant later, shuddering all over, and Mal let himself go. After so much teasing, his orgasm seemed to go on and on. He had time to drop his head against Lucy's neck and whimper her name.

They lay perfectly still for a moment, and then Lucy panted, "Well…it's been a while since I've done it like that. Get off me."

Mal backed off of her and turned instantly into a cat. "We…ah…don't have to—"

"Ever talk about this again," Lucy finished for him. "Excellent."

Mal felt dazed. He was still trying to understand what Lucy had just given him. "Am I still cloaking?"

Lucy melted into her dragon form. She examined his aura. "Yes. It should last for a while."

"Are you…alright? I feel like I've got a lot of your magic inside me."

Lucy yawned. "I'm a little tired."

Mal snorted. "Me, too. Maybe for different reasons."

The fire on the beach had burned down to almost nothing. Lucy gave it a puff of flame. Then she stretched out beside it. Mal curled up against her back. For an instant, he thought she would tell him to go lie on the other side of the fire.

Then she stood up, turned around, and lay down beside him, facing in the opposite direction. She draped her long neck over his hips, and after a moment, Mal tucked his nose against her flank. He knew he couldn't really sleep in the dream space, but he felt content enough to let his mind drift, almost to doze.

They were still lying curled together when a wolf and a fox came trotting up the beach.

43

Azrael

Azrael woke alone in his bed. He blinked and felt dust in his eyes, just for a moment. He raised his hand above his face, saw the silver on his finger, and remembered *everything*.

Azrael sat straight up in bed, snarling. He turned to the headboard and saw the words he'd scribbled each morning—messages to himself in the few frantic seconds when he partially understood what was happening to him: Something is feeding on

"Me," Azrael finished the sentence aloud. He felt the chill of those words in his bones. With a sinking feeling, he reached for his own magic.

He recoiled instantly. It was worse here than in the dream—an oily contamination that made his own power feel untrustworthy and alien, a weapon that might twist in his hand. *I am halfway to possession.* The ring was, for the moment, an untainted source of his own magic and a connection to Jessica. Even that anchor, however, would not hold for long. He would have only a few moments in full possession of his faculties. He had to make the most of them.

Azrael sprang out of bed. In spite of the precariousness of his situation, he did not feel anxious. He felt light with rage. *He hurt Mal and Jessica. He stole Lucy. He intended to make the* murder of my friends a mere footnote to a broader massacre. *By all the gods, I will have blood!*

But first, to deal with that vile book.

"Tod?" Azrael didn't see him in the room, so he glanced under the bed. The wolf lay there, fast asleep with his head on his paws. Azrael considered trying to wake him. *But what if Jessica needs him right now?*

Tod couldn't do what Azrael needed anyway. He was too human, too mortal, too good. *Time to fight fire with fire.*

Azrael couldn't leave his bedroom. He didn't trust himself to walk past the dreamcatcher on the kitchen table. His supply of untainted magic was pitifully small, and he had precious few materials. He needed a sacrifice, and he didn't have much in the way of conventional options, except perhaps Tod's lifeblood, and he wasn't about to offer that.

Azrael had one other option, however. He could offer himself.

He'd never summoned a demon this way before, never dared, but he did not hesitate now. He drew the simplest possible summoning circle on his bedroom floor, using the same pen he'd been using to scribble on his headboard. He activated the circle with a trace of magic from the ring. No need for salt. He wasn't trying to protect himself.

Azrael stood before the circle and intoned, "Cleothrasis Andramache Stigorath Tash, I summon you. By your true name, I bind you. I offer myself as sacrifice. Come to me and do my will."

Some distant part of Azrael's brain wondered at his own audacity. He'd infused the name with as much magic as he dared, but his power was weak, and he knew it. For this sort of summoning to work, the sacrifice itself had to be very strong.

For an interminable moment, nothing happened. Then a red plume rose in the middle of the circle—the thinnest stream of smoke, as though the boards of his bedroom were on fire. The smoke twisted in the air, licking towards him like a questing tongue. Azrael put out his fingers and let the smoke drift through them. Instantly, it blossomed into form.

The creature that appeared in the middle of the circle was deceptively small. To all appearances, she was a child of perhaps seven or eight, sitting cross-legged. Her mouse-brown hair bobbed in messy ponytails on either side of her head, tied with different colored ribbons. She was barefoot, dressed in a stained, pale pink jumper. At first glance, her eyes were the only unsettling thing about her. They were red as blood.

"Lord Azrael," she cooed. "It has been such a long time. You're all grown up!"

"And you're exactly the same. Cleo, I need you to go into the next room, close a book for me, and bind it. The book is something like a spirit vessel, and it will try to devour you. It has already trapped three demons. I believe it contains an entity, and I believe it is a dark aspect. I don't know which one."

The girl clapped her hands and stood up. "And you're so angry about it! Delicious! But there's something wrong with you, isn't there?"

"It has been feeding on me," he admitted. "You may consume its magic out of my aura, but I forbid you to use that magic without my explicit command. I forbid you to possess or control me or to influence my decisions. Once my aura is free of dark magic, you must cease feeding on me."

Cloe pouted. "You're always so picky."

Azrael rolled his eyes. "Can you consume this magic?"

"Oh, yes. I can do all kinds of things with this!"

"Then please go close the book."

"Is Mal inside?" she asked sweetly.

"Yes."

Cleo and Mal had always gotten along, but Azrael was under no delusions about Cleo's loyalty or sense of friendship. She was dark aspected Wrath—an agent of pure chaos.

"No wonder you're so pissed! Never fret, Master. I'll go disembowel something and be right back."

"Metaphorically, please," he called after her. "I don't want the book destroyed until I get my people back."

44

Jessica

"Mal! Lucy!" Jessica dashed forward over the sand. It still felt strange to be so low to the ground.

Mal leapt to his feet. Lucy raised her head, stretched, and addressed herself to Jessica. "Darling, I thought you'd never get here. Please reassure your lover of your safety. He has been fairly gnawing his own tail with anxiety."

Mal stared at Jessica—at the red fox, fluffed with excitement. *Please still love me.*

"Jessica?"

"Mal."

He made a noise somewhere between a sigh and sob and butted her so hard with his head that he knocked her over. Then he was a man, scooping her off the ground, clutching her to his chest. "Jessica! Oh gods, I thought you were lost in the void! I thought you'd come unraveled! I thought you were dying all alone." He stopped to catch his breath. "Why are you so small?"

Lucy huffed. "Because she's only a little bit of a demon. If you stop crushing her, she might talk to you."

Mal really was holding her too tightly. Jessica squirmed. "I almost did come apart," she managed. "I changed shape to get out of the void, but I didn't know who I was, and I came out in a different dream, and I probably would have just wandered around until I fell apart, except that Tod came looking for me.

And then he found Azrael and led him back to me, and it's all very complicated, but we're alright."

Behind them, Lucy said, "Hello. It's Tod, isn't it?"

"That's me. You're Lucy?"

"Yes, we met briefly at one of Mal's dissolute parties. You're not a demon; what on earth are you doing here?"

"Well, I have several friends who are demons— Omph!"

Mal dropped to his knees beside the wolf and hugged him with the arm that wasn't holding Jessica.

"You are the best werewolf I know."

"I'm the only werewolf you know."

"And my favorite. Have I ever told you that your magic is delicious? Even secondhand?"

"That is something I never needed to know, Mal."

Jessica giggled in Mal's other arm. "I told Tod that now we're *really* Red and the Wolf."

Mal barked a laugh. "How come you don't turn into a human?" he asked Jessica.

"Because I'm naked! I can't make clothes like you. Apparently it takes a lot of practice."

"So?"

"So I'd rather not feel any more vulnerable here than I already do. It's also sort of hard for me to change shape. That takes practice, too, apparently. Ren helped me. I don't want to get stuck naked as a human."

Mal's fingers had encountered the slender circlet around her neck. "What's this?"

"It's my ring. It changes when I change just like your collar, only it wouldn't stay on my foot." Jessica licked his face. "We're getting married! That's alright with you, isn't it?"

"Of course! Azrael said that?"

"Yes. He made rings out of a link of your collar." She leaned up and whispered in Mal's ear, "We're going to have a baby."

He stared at her wide-eyed. "He *said* that?"

Jessica tried to nod. That felt strange as a fox, so she wagged her tail instead.

Mal laughed with delight.

"He was so scared, Mal, but he said yes."

"And you said yes."

"Everyone said yes! All yes!"

Mal kissed her on the nose. "Well, now I really can't die in here."

"I told you Azrael would get it all straightened out," began Lucy and stopped. She turned towards the sea, her long, fine-boned face alert.

A moment later, Jessica heard it, too—a diminution of the waves. The fog over the water had thickened. Jessica could no longer see the ocean.

Tod took a cautious step into the mist. Then another. And another.

"Tod?" called Jessica uncertainly.

He came hurrying back. "The ocean's turning into void."

Lucy growled.

"What does that mean?" asked Mal.

"It means that someone is shrinking the dream space," said Lucy.

"And what does *that* mean?"

"I think it means this is about to be over. One way or the other."

A moment later, the fog began to thicken over the beach, smothering Lucy's fire. "The sand is changing," said Tod.

"We're being driven inland," murmured Lucy. "One guess as to where."

"What happens if we just stay here?" asked Mal.

Lucy shook her head. "In a dream void? We could get trapped. I think we'd better play along for now." She gave a full-body dragon stretch and then led the way into the hedge maze.

45

Azrael

Two hours later, Azrael was in his garden, examining his own recent endeavors. He was grudgingly impressed. *My enemy is clever.* He was still trying to decide how to deal with the problem when his butler approached hesitantly to inform him that his guests had arrived.

"Which guests?"

The butler was eyeing Cleo, who stood on one leg, grubby hands twisted behind her back and somehow still radiating malevolence. In the light of day, the stains on her jumper might have been mud…or they might have been something else. The longer one looked at them, the less they resembled mud.

"The group who were to arrive early," said the butler, eyes darting between Azrael and Cleo. "Lord Loudain, the Lady who goes by S, and a gentleman who only gave the name Jacob. Lady S also has a lemur with her, my lord."

Azrael massaged his temples. He'd lost track of time during his possession. *This was a narrow miss. Just as well they're here, though. They've got some explaining to do.* Indeed, he was almost as anxious to get his hands on the High Council as he was to get his hands on this rogue sorcerer.

"Show them into an audience chamber," said Azrael to the servant. "Provide them with refreshment. Put their luggage in their rooms. And Micah…"

The man went still at the mention of his name. "My lord?"

"I've been dealing with something very bad for the last few days. It is almost over. Please tell the rest of the staff that there's no need to be…concerned."

Micah's posture visibly loosened. "This is good to hear, my lord."

Azrael gave the staff some time to see his guests into the audience chamber. He visited his tower and picked up a few supplies—half-finished spells that required only a little magic to activate.

At last, he squared his shoulders, straightened his cravat—red to match Cleo's eyes—and marched into the audience chamber. Two men and a woman sat in comfortable chairs around a cut-glass table, sipping drinks and talking. Lord Loudain—Tod's grandfather—was easily the most imposing. He was a big, square-jawed man, mostly bald, his fringe of red hair frosted white, with streaks of silver in his neatly trimmed beard. He wore a sword and looked very capable of using it. Lady S was a middle-aged woman, slightly plump, with dark hair and a freckled nose that crinkled when she smiled. She wore her lemur demon like a stole. The demon himself had a silver collar studded with blue and green gemstones. Jacob—who was not actually a council member, but merely a consultant—sat a little apart from the other two. He was a lanky man with sharp features, salt and pepper hair, and dark brown eyes that missed nothing.

A few weeks ago, Azrael had envisioned a pleasant meeting here—a few uncomfortable questions, reassurances on all sides, discussion of what to expect from the rest of the Council, then a tour. He'd intended to make nice with these people as he'd never done before.

Well, that's right out. Azrael entered the room, Cleo on his heels, and instantly both doors shut, locks clicked into place, and invisible wards engaged. The lemur on Lady S's shoulder managed one hiss before Azrael sucked all sound out of the room. The three magicians leapt to their feet with what would have been cries of alarm, except that the room had gone as quiet as the bottom of the sea. At the same time, the lamps dimmed, shadows leapt and darkened. Cleo giggled at his side, although

Azrael only caught the motion and no noise. One of the stains on the front of her jumper had become unmistakably a bloody handprint.

The three magicians stood mute. Loudain had drawn his sword, Lady S had pulled something that looked like a wand out of her purse, and Jacob had thrust both hands into the pockets of his jacket. Under other circumstances, any of these three would have made a formidable opponent. But not here. Here they were in Azrael's territory.

"You can put those toys away," he said into the unnatural silence. "My wards tend to react badly with the magic of other magicians. Fatally, in fact. I am not here to attack you, but I *am* going to get some answers. I have had one hell of a week, *colleagues*. Someone is trying to use me as a murder weapon to annihilate you and the rest of the council. This person is a skilled dream-walker. He has obviously been well-trained, and he has a vendetta. I find it difficult to believe that the High Mage Council did not know about him or anticipate such an attack. I find it offensive that I was not warned. This sort of chicanery is exactly why I dislike dealing with other magicians. *You* brought this to my island. My people have suffered and are still suffering as a result. I do not appreciate being put in the middle of other people's squabbles without my consent, and I highly resent being used as puppet!"

"Do we get to talk, or are you only going to shout at us?" The voice was Jacob's. Of course it was Jacob's. Azrael resisted the urge to demand to know how he'd done it.

"Talk," he spat and released the spell of silence.

Loudain gave an audible inhalation.

"Hello to you, too," drawled Lady S's lemur.

"Maybe you should not greet the rest of the council with a dark aspect of Wrath on your heels," said Lady S. "If I could offer some advice, I'd start there."

Azrael snorted. "My lady, if I don't get some answers at once, the council will definitely not like my greeting. I'll give them a real reason to call me a dark sorcerer."

Loudain stepped between Azrael, Lady S, and her bristling demon. "Please calm down," he said in his deep rumble. "We're all on the same side here. Azrael, where are your two bright magic creatures? Where are Mal and Jessica?"

"Taken," snarled Azrael. "Trapped in a spirit vessel that is feeding on their magic. It was supposed to wipe my memories of them and direct me to build a gate that will summon a creature to kill you. It almost worked."

A moment's silence. Loudain licked his lips. "Please tell us the whole story. Let us help."

Jacob's perfectly controlled expression revealed nothing when he said, "Did it take Lucrecia?"

"Of course it took Lucy!" snapped Azrael. "It took every demon who came near it!"

"Except that one," said Lady S, still looking distrustfully at Cleo.

"She's a dark aspect," said Jacob quietly. "The creature providing power for the vessel is probably dark aspected as well?" He directed this at Azrael, who nodded. "It's easier to fight dark magic with dark magic," finished Jacob.

"Perhaps easier," began Lady S, "but—"

"Let us not judge what Lord Azrael has done until we understand his position," said Loudain. "Azrael?"

"First, I want to know who is attacking me. I cannot believe you have no idea who it is."

The three magicians looked at each other. "Chester?" ventured Lady S.

"He'd never do something like this," muttered Loudain. "He's no dream-walker, either. What about Carlisle?"

"Not her style at all," said Jacob.

"Are you certain that you weren't the target?" said Lady S to Azrael. "Plenty of people don't like *you*."

"I am aware of that," said Azrael. "And, yes, I am certain."

"I agree with Loudain," said Jacob. "You need to tell us what happened. Trust that we are not fools and that we really have no immediate idea of who is doing this. Give us more information."

Azrael looked between them. He felt so frustrated with all this dithering. Dimly, he was aware that Cleo was probably making his reaction worse. Like Mal, she stirred up the vice on which she fed. He should tell her to stop. But dear gods, feeling angry felt so much better than feeling afraid.

Loudain cleared his throat. "The longer you wait, the less chance we'll have of retrieving your…"

Azrael glared at him. *If you say 'creatures' again…*

"People," finished Loudain.

Azrael shut his eyes, took a deep breath. "I think you should have a look at my garden."

46

Azrael

Azrael gave them a rapid-fire version of events as they walked through the palace and grounds in the crisp, wintery afternoon. He didn't mention the exact circumstances under which he'd broken the dreamcatcher's encryption charm, but there was no way to avoid the fact that Mal and Jessica slept in his bed. He didn't mention anything about babies, but the engagement rings were a critical piece of the story. He didn't give the werewolf's name—although he was certain Loudain guessed—but there was no way to avoid the fact that one of his wards was a werewolf.

Azrael was coming to the end of the story when he realized exactly how much he was revealing under the influence of Cleo's reckless fury and his own desperation. He faltered. To his surprise, Lady S—whom Azrael knew and trusted the least—came forward and looped her arm through his. "It's alright."

"It really isn't," said the lemur from her shoulder. "This book has forced you to do an appalling amount of work. I am sickened, simply sickened!"

Azrael laughed in spite of himself. He glanced at the lemur. "I don't believe we have been introduced." *You are obviously Sloth, but who else?*

"I call him Amos," said Lady S. "He's very relaxing. Would you like him to counter the effects of your minion of incandescent rage?"

"No, thank you," said Azrael. After a moment, he added, "I've summoned Cleo before, but only briefly, and it's been more than a decade. She's not a usual part of my household."

"We laid waste to an army once!" piped up Cleo.

"She's often underestimated," put in Jacob. "I know of two sorcerers in the last fifty years who have summoned her and lost control of her."

"Jacob, Jacob," piped Cleo, "you sent me home once."

"I did."

"Are you going to send me home now?"

"Not yet."

"You know I'll lead you all to a grisly death," she continued in her child's voice.

"No, you will not," said Azrael. "I'll send you home quite soon. In the meantime, there is something that needs killing, and you like that."

"I do!"

"Then be patient and stay a while longer."

She giggled. "You're just angry because they took Mal. I wonder if he will even remember you once you get him out of the book. He might have unraveled, you know—waiting for you to come, thinking you'd abandoned him. He might be just a shell of magic, all hollowed out with nothing—"

"Cleo, shut up," said Azrael.

Loudain gave him a clap on the shoulder opposite Lady S. "She's Wrath, my friend. She's going to keep saying whatever will keep you angry."

"Azrael," said Lady S, "I know you would not choose to reveal quite this much about your private business if you thought you had any choice. However, you brought us here early, presumably because you trusted us. Assume that trust was well-placed."

Azrael relaxed a fraction.

"Actually," said Loudain, "I think you might consider making your personal arrangements more widely known. At least then people won't think you indulge yourself with all of these courtiers."

Azrael was momentarily speechless. "They think I sleep with the courtiers?"

"What did you expect them to think?"

"Well, I—" Azrael was indignant. "I don't."

Jacob spoke quietly. "I find that mundanes and even many magicians suppose that sorcerers are prone to the vice of the creature they most often employ. This is simply a misunderstanding, probably because sorcerers are so rare. In my experience, we work best with creatures who are most unlike ourselves. It's easier to ward against them. Lady S, for instance, is one of the most industrious people I know."

Lady S spoke again. "Mal sleeps with the courtiers?"

"Sometimes," said Azrael, "if they're amenable. More often, they get involved with each other and he feeds indirectly. They entertain political guests, which gives me a way to exert influence. The volunteers do know that sex will be expected. Mal must be fed. I create a sensuous environment, but I don't force anyone to do anything. It wouldn't help if I did. Mal wouldn't feed."

Lady S patted his arm reassuringly.

Azrael couldn't decide whether he was sharing too much or not enough. He wasn't accustomed to explaining himself. "I don't even go to the orgies," he offered. "Mal keeps pestering me to go lately. He says he just wants me to be friendly and play games—"

He broke off when he realized that Loudain was laughing. "I'm sorry," he said when he got himself under control. "I've never heard anyone talk about orgies as though they were afternoon bingo."

Azrael wasn't sure how to respond to this, so he said, "Since you've all been privy to intimate details of my life, can we not pretend that you don't have a vested interest in getting my people back safely? Loudain, we both know why you should care. Jacob, I believe you have more than casual interest in getting Lucy back in one piece. And I believe Lady S and Amos wanted Mal and I to help them figure some things out."

"We will do our best to help you get them back," said Jacob quietly.

They reached the hedge maze and stood in silence for a moment, staring at the elaborate summoning circle Azrael had drawn in spelled chalk. The dreamcatcher lay on a picnic table nearby, bound and warded. Nothing was getting into that book now. Unfortunately, nothing was getting out, either.

"This isn't really a summoning circle," murmured Lady S as she walked around the edges. "This is a gate."

Azrael nodded. "That's what the sorcerer called it, too. I think my delusion was meant to make me think I was summoning a creature whose name I knew. However, I was, in fact, intended to open a gate to a creature over which I had no control."

"Was there no map?" asked Loudain as he examined the runes around the edges. "No anchors?"

Azrael shook his head. "I think it opens into dream space. That's why it looks so strange."

Jacob was examining the dreamcatcher. "I think this is the anchor. You've built the lock, and this is the key."

"Can you tell what kind of demon it is, Jay?" asked Loudain.

"Dark aspect for sure," muttered Jacob. "Azrael, can I use magic here?"

"I'd rather you didn't. I was going to build an airlock for guests to learn what parts of their magical signature might be compatible with mine. That was right before all this happened. Instead of building an airlock, I built this damn gate."

Lady S rolled her eyes. "Oh for gods sake's. It's Pride!" She gestured at Azrael. "Half the council thought he *was* Pride until he came to his trial. Nothing else would have such an easy time feeding on him. Do not look at me like that, Lord Azrael. I am right."

Azrael jammed his hands in his pockets. "I'm sure you are."

Jacob nodded. "Dark aspects of Pride are terrifying. They're not often summoned." He coughed. "They uh...tend to have an easy time feeding on magicians in general. It's difficult to properly ward against them."

"Who is doing this?" demanded Azrael. "Are you really none the wiser?"

Loudain and Lady S looked at each other. "The memory magic," began Loudain, "the dream-walking, the circus…"

"She's dead!" exclaimed Lady S. "I saw her down the river myself. She is dead."

"Who?" demanded Azrael.

"Lady Zersic," said Jacob.

"I heard the Council executed her," said Azrael.

"We did," said Lady S. "People were disappearing at her circus. She'd gotten more eccentric over the years. Her demons were running wild. She'd been warned multiple times, but nothing changed. We received proof of one of the killings and that was enough."

"Did she have friends or relatives who might want revenge?"

Lady S shook her head. "She'd cut herself off from everyone except her demons."

"Apprentice?" said Jacob quietly.

Loudain hesitated. "We heard there was an apprentice…"

"We heard a rumor," objected Lady S. "We never found any evidence to support it. If he existed, he died in the fire."

Azrael stared at her. "You killed a woman with a dependent?"

Amos rolled his eyes dramatically from his mistress's shoulder. "We killed a dark sorceress with an apprentice. Maybe. Probably not."

"A woman with a dependent," repeated Azrael.

Lady S shrugged. "She was a murderer. Anyone she trained would have been a murderer, too."

Loudain nodded. "Demons were in control of Zersic, not the other way around. The Council doesn't execute people lightly. I suspect that if they'd found an apprentice, they would have sent him down the river after his mistress." He scratched his head. "This seems too advanced for an apprentice in any case."

"Maybe she got away," said Lady S helplessly. "Maybe Zersic isn't as dead as we thought. She certainly has motive to attack the council and the right skill set to create this trap. But nobody suspects she survived, Azrael. No one saw this coming, I promise you."

Azrael nodded. He felt he'd learned all he could from these people. He wasn't sure it would be enough. "Cleo, I think you should take your other form now."

Cleo looked up from where she'd been drawing dismembered bodies in the dirt. "Why?"

"Just a hunch."

Cleo shrugged. She melted into something that looked like a weasel the size of a cocker spaniel, still with alarmingly red eyes. She was, in fact, a mongoose. She zipped around Azrael's legs like an excited squirrel. "Let's go kill something! Or get you killed! I don't care which!"

"What are you going to do?" asked Jacob.

"Go after my people."

"You're going to open the gate?"

"Yes. Would you like me to give you time to get off the island?"

Loudain drew his sword. "Of course not."

Azrael looked at him skeptically, but Lady S spoke at once. "Of course we're coming with you, Azrael. Give us a little credit."

"You do know that the sorcerer will be waiting, right?" said Jacob. "When you bound the book, you certainly triggered alarms. He'll know something has gone wrong."

"I am aware," said Azrael. "*You* know that you may not be able to use your own magic, right? Even in the dream space? The book is still on my island, and you may still be blocked by my wards."

"I think that's a chance we have to take," said Lady S. "Especially if the alternative is never knowing whether you've become a puppet of dark magic."

Azrael nodded grudgingly. "Alright then. Let's open a dream gate."

47

Azrael

The four magicians stood around the edge of the circle. Azrael placed the dreamcatcher in the center and drew the final runes. For a moment, nothing happened. Then Azrael noted a disturbance in the air over the circle—a shimmer like heat or the ripples from a pebble tossed into a still lake. The effect was unlike any gate Azrael had ever seen. It was, in fact, very like opening a pocket world in his charmed picture frame.

Fog rose from the ground inside the circle and began drifting through the garden. "Gods below," murmured Amos. "This gate is making the whole fabric of the mortal plane unstable. This is going to be a thin spot for a long time. Are you sure you don't want to cut your losses and burn the book?"

"He's right," said Cleo from Azrael's feet. "Any smart person would just torch the thing and be done. What was the point of getting your mind back if you're just going to open the gate anyway?"

Azrael did not bother to answer. He concentrated on the rolling fog. He could not see the ground anymore. *I'm coming Mal, Jessica, Lucy.*

He reached, cautiously, for his own magic and found that it was untainted. Relief washed through him, but only for an instant. His supply was pitifully small. He had not performed the necessary spells to be able to draw on Cleo. There hadn't been time. He could command her, but not use her magic. Like most sorcerers, Azrael had a great capacity for holding and channeling magic, but very little ability to create it. On his own, he was the weakest of all magicians.

Azrael pulled the collar from under his shirt. *If I can just get this on Mal...* The collar might bring Mal back to himself, even if he'd lost his memories. It would allow Azrael to use his magic. If he had any left to give.

But even if he doesn't, Lucy might. Azrael had her bottle in his pocket, which meant he could use her magic. Lucy was extremely powerful when she first emerged from her bottle, but she tired quickly. Azrael wasn't sure how tired she was likely to be after days in a demon-eating spirit vessel. Surely not fresh.

Even if I can't use magic at all, Mal and Lucy are deadly in a fight. Cleo is fresh from the astral plane. We should be able to do this.

If... whispered a voice in his head. *If, if, if.*

The fog cleared a little. Azrael saw that the ground inside the circle had disappeared, along with the dreamcatcher. He was looking through a hole into a twilit, foggy world. He saw a round platform, dark water moving in an enormous basin beneath, broken flagstones beyond. Something glided briefly across his field of vision, silhouetted against the paler flagstones.

Azrael stepped into the circle. "Mal!" Cleo bounded in after him. The act of entering the circle appeared to drop them about ten feet without any sensation of falling. The brilliant halo of light from the garden shone overhead. Azrael found himself standing on the platform in the middle of a broad basin, perhaps twenty feet off the ground. Broken flagstones surrounded the basin and beyond them, a wall of dark green hedge.

Faces that he'd feared he would never see again looked up at him—Mal with his paws on the edge of the basin, Lucy in dragon form beyond him, Jessica and Tod a little further out, running back and forth. They were all trying to talk at once.

Azrael heard Lucy shout, "Mal, get down! Have you lost your mind? It eats magic!"

Mal was leaning as far out as he could over the dark water. "Azrael!"

Azrael wanted to say so many things. *I didn't put you here. I would never. I love you. I've missed you so much.* But there was no time for that.

"Where's my collar?" bellowed Mal.

Azrael held it out, leaning over the water. The gap was too great. "Shall I throw it?"

"No!" exclaimed Mal. "Lucy is right; the water eats magic. It's some kind of vortex. It—"

Azrael interrupted him. "Lucy, come get it!"

Lucy spread her wings, but she'd only taken one beat into the air when an invisible force hit her like a gunshot and she came down hard on the flagstones. That was when Jacob stepped into the circle. "Lucrecia!"

"Oh!" exclaimed Cleo at Azrael's side. "That's interesting."

"What?"

"Her aura's gone clear," said Cleo.

Azrael felt sick. Lucy had been hit with a spell that had obliterated her will. He had a good idea of where that spell must have come from. "It's the sorcerer. He's got one hell of a binding spell. It may not hold a demon forever without a name, but it's enough to knock them out of a fight. Lucy!"

Lucy raised her head, her expression vacant and confused.

Azrael whipped out her bottle and depressed the bulb. Lucy melted into golden mist, flowing back into the bottle. She was out of the fight, but she was safe.

Loudain stepped onto the platform. "I take it we can't touch the water?"

"No, it's dark magic," said Jacob. He opened his palm, and Azrael saw that he was holding a partially finished spell. He whispered to it.

Azrael winced. *I guess we'll find out if my wards are in effect here.*

The spell flared to life. It didn't backfire, didn't incinerate Jacob. But it was weak—a wavering flame where Azrael suspected there should have been a fireball. "Azrael, why do you have to be so damned good at wards?" asked Jacob irritably.

"Are his wards still blocking us?" asked Loudain.

"Dampening," muttered Jacob.

"Well, I don't have much to contribute unless I can get this collar on Mal," said Azrael.

"The water!" Lady S's voice seemed to come from a great way off and then abruptly from quite close as she stepped into the circle. "It's the demon!"

Azrael had already noticed that something was happening to the water. It appeared to be growing thicker, more viscous, congealing into lumps and smooth curves. Below him, Mal ran back and forth along the edge of the fountain, growling. Tod and Jessica were standing back-to-back, bristling.

"Cleo, can you see the sorcerer?" asked Azrael.

Cleo would be looking at auras, which should be visible even in dark places. "Over there."

Azrael looked where she indicated, but saw only fog and shadows. *I need to strike hard. We will win this fight quickly or not at all.* Still, Azrael hesitated. He wanted answers. He wanted revenge. He wanted resolution, which would include an explanation of how these spells had been created. However, he also wanted Mal, Jessica, and Tod to be safe as quickly as possible.

"Go kill him, Cleo." It was a direct command, a compulsion that was also in line with Cleo's nature. She launched herself joyfully from the platform in a flying leap that did not touch the water, if water it could still be called.

As Cleo hit the ground, Azrael saw the first coil. It did not so much rise out of the water as resolve out of it—glistening black scales on a loop of muscular body as big around as a tree trunk. Jacob shouted, "Try not to look at it!" and then hurled magic at the monster that was rising out of the fountain.

Meanwhile, Cleo bounded across the flagstones like a deadly terrier, charged into the shadows…and was flung back. She toppled head over tail to land in a graceless sprawl at the edge of the marble bowl.

Azrael stared at her, horrified.

The sorcerer finally slouched out of the fog, "So you came after all," he said to Azrael. "That's weird. And you brought a weasel."

Azrael clenched his fists. He could feel the fireball forming in his hand, prepared to blast this brat down the river. But he wasn't sure it would work. He had so little magic.

Amos hissed from Lady S's shoulder, and the kid added, "Two weasels."

Mal was coming around the edge of the fountain towards the sorcerer in a predatory stalk. Tod was approaching on the other side. *If this kid could take Lucy out… If he could knock Cleo down, fresh from the astral plane…*

Around Azrael, his fellow magicians had flung up a desperate shield against the attacking serpent demon. Amos's collar and Loudain's sword were glowing as brightly as the fragment of sky above their heads. "It takes ten times as much magic to do anything here," grated Lady S, "and that thing is well-fed. This shield is not going to hold for long."

"Look, I grew up playing with demons," continued the enemy sorcerer to Azrael as he watched Mal approach. "If I didn't know how to defend myself, I wouldn't be here. But, hey, you beat my memory charm somehow, so congrats. I'm really glad you decided to open my gate anyway, though. Otherwise, I would have had to start all over again, and I'm not sure I have enough potatoes. Thanks for bringing a snack for Chewy."

A triangular head the size of a rowboat reared up beside their platform. The forked tongue that licked out to taste their wards was as big around as a human forearm. Loudain grunted suddenly and dropped his sword.

"Don't look it in the eyes!" roared Jacob. "Saline, help him!"

Loudain had dropped to his knees, muttering and fumbling. Lady S knelt beside him. "Listen to me, your name is Alistair Loudain. Look at your focus. No, here. Look at it."

Jacob was holding up the ward by himself now, and Azrael could see that he was struggling. The snake struck. It bounced off a wall that became briefly visible—a twisting shape of runes and magic. The shield dented on impact, flaring and sparking. In desperation, Azrael threw what little magic he possessed into

Jacob's ward. Blue fire lanced up through silver runes, lacing them back together, straightening the shield. The snake struck again, gave a scream like a raptor's. The wall flickered.

Azrael spared a glance at the ground. The sorcerer was looking at Mal. Azrael couldn't tell whether he'd seen Tod. *Can Mal stand up to that binding spell?* Azrael wanted to believe that he could. He wanted to.

Azrael jumped down from the platform. He knew it was going to hurt. He didn't have any magic left to cushion his fall onto marble. Fortunately, he did have a giant snake. Azrael landed on the beast without breaking his legs, heard its outraged hiss, and vaulted over the side of the fountain before its lashing could crush him.

He staggered to his feet, feeling the jarring pain in his legs. He saw Mal, perhaps twenty yards away, and held out the collar. "Mal!"

Everything happened at once. Mal changed directions, running towards Azrael instead of the sorcerer. Tod charged just as the sorcerer flung out a hand towards him. "No one invited you to this party, asshole! Wake up!"

Tod vanished.

Overhead, Azrael could hear the teeth-jarring note of wards straining and breaking.

Mal was ten yards away, five.

He went sprawling.

The enemy sorcerer collapsed to one knee, grunting with the recoil of his own spell. He got up swearing. "Fucking werewolf. I'm going to find it and shoot it when I get out of here. Bloody fuck. You, cat demon, come here. Guard me."

Azrael stared at Mal. They were mere paces apart. Azrael was holding out the collar. "Mal, put your head through it. We can still win. Just come to me. Please."

Mal look at him for an instant longer. Then he blinked and looked away.

"Forget him," said the sorcerer. "Kill him if he comes near you. Come to me, kitty."

Mal came.

Azrael took one more step after him, but Jacob's voice range out sharply from above. "Azrael, his aura…"

He means it's gone clear, thought Azrael. *Like Lucy's.*

Out of the corner of his eye, he saw Jessica dragging Cleo away from the edge of the basin. The mongoose was still limp. *Did he kill her? If he could kill Cleo…* "Forget him."

Azrael thought that he'd come back to himself only to understand, fully and cruelly, what he was losing. To talk to Jessica about futures and weddings and babies, to see Mal in his right mind one last time. *I should have said the rest of what I wanted to say. I should have just shouted it.*

Mal stopped in front of the sorcerer. "Tell me your name, beast, so that I can bind you properly." Azrael's heart sank into his shoes.

Mal hesitated. His voice came out small and confused. "I…I don't think I'm supposed to."

"You are." The kid was looking at him and through him, examining his aura and magical signature. He looked over Mal's head at Azrael. "Did no one ever tell you you're supposed to bind them? Shit man, it's like leaving money on the ground. Speak up, demon. Your name."

Mal took a breath. Even the snake paused its attack to listen. "Did no one ever tell you," said Mal softly, "that demons *lie?*"

The kid looked confused. He started to say something.

Then Mal melted into black smoke and poured *into* him.

Azrael shouted. So did Jacob. Then Azrael was running towards the kid, who was clawing at his face. Smoke continued to rush in through his eyes, nose, and mouth. He began to scream—a gurgling shriek, the like of which Azrael hoped to never hear again.

Something flashed past Azrael in a blur of dark brown. *Cleo!* "The snake!" he had time to bark. "Cleo, kill the snake!"

Cleo changed directions, seemingly in midair, and hurled herself at the enormous reptile. There was a tremendous thumping and hissing. Azrael had the impression that the snake had slithered out of the bowl of the fountain, but he didn't have time to worry about that. He'd reached the sorcerer, who stood swaying, hands at his sides now, eyes dilated to pools of night.

Azrael heard Jacob's rapid footsteps behind him. "Once a demon starts doing that—"

"Jacob, shut up." Azrael kept his eyes on the kid's. "Mal, get out of him. Right now. Come on."

The kid looked down at his hands, turned them over as though he'd never seen them before. This was true possession. Mal had never been inside a human—not like this.

Jacob was at Azrael's elbow. "He'll be both of them and neither of them in just a moment. We have only a few seconds to deal with this."

To kill him, you mean. "Mal," whispered Azrael. He could hear the catch in his voice and he didn't care. "Come back to me. Please."

The sorcerer's muddy eyes met his. And flashed green.

Black smoke boiled out of the man's eyes, nose, and mouth. The condensing mass hit the broken pavers just as the sorcerer crumpled. Then Mal was in Azrael's arms—human, solid, shaking with terror and relief. "I was so scared!"

"I know." Azrael wrapped his arms around Mal's warmth and weight, buried a hand in his hair. "It's alright, it's alright. *We're* alright."

He heard a whine near his feet. "Jessica. Gods, I'm sorry. If you want to be human, I'll loan you my coat."

"Or I'll just be naked, too," offered Mal, "and then half of the people will stare at me and not you. Naked, except for this." He snatched the collar out of Azrael's hand and tossed it over his head.

Jessica laughed and then all three of them were hugging. "I gave Cleo some magic and woke her up. She seems sweet."

"Only you would describe Wrath as sweet," muttered Azrael. "Thank you for getting her up."

"She and the snake are having quite a fight," continued Jessica. "Do you think she needs help?"

"Doubt it," said Azrael.

He was right.

48

Azrael

Mal was replete with magic. Azrael wanted to ask how that was possible. He wanted to ask when Mal had learned to cloak. He wanted to ask so many things. *But first we have to finish this.*

The sorcerer was still flat on the ground when Azrael hit him with a binding spell that was *not* just for demons. He curled up like a leaf before an open flame. In the same moment, Mal said, "His name is Nicholas Horatio Holloway."

Azrael and Jacob both looked at Mal in surprise. "I was inside his head for at least ten seconds. What did you think I was doing?"

"Jacob thought you were preparing to become the new Dark Lord of the Shattered Sea," said Azrael with the smallest amount of sarcasm he could manage.

Jacob shrugged. "It's what most demons would do with a sorcerer's body."

"I've already got a sorcerer," said Mal.

Jacob looked at him skeptically. "I see that."

Beyond the fountain, Cleo and the snake were dodging and striking at each other. Loudain was on his feet again, watching the spectacle with Lady S and Amos. Cleo finally managed to tear a piece out of the snake's throat. Black ichor spattered the broken flagstones.

Azrael shrugged out of his coat and handed it to Jessica. It came to her knees. "Speaking of sorcerer's bodies," she said, "he's not really here, is he? Can't he just wake up and get away?"

"Yes and no," said Jacob. "Maintaining a dream space like this means spending a lot of time here. He'll have created safeguards to prevent himself from waking in the middle of something important. He has locked himself into the dream, and he can't wake unless he removes the locks."

"Well, that's convenient for us," said Mal. "Bind him and leave him here."

The kid did not look up.

Mal gave him a nudge with his foot. "Leave him here and let the dream collapse. He can languish in the void until his body dies or he unravels and goes mad. He can learn what that feels like."

Azrael heard a soft thump and turned to see that Loudain and Lady S had jumped down from the platform, cushioned by magic, and were coming towards them. "Well, this looks like it's wrapping up," said Lady S.

"How are you feeling, Loudain?" asked Azrael.

"I'm fine," growled the old man. "Godsdamned demon just took a bite out of me, that's all."

"Nothing injured but your pride?" asked Jacob with the hint of a smile.

Loudain huffed. "Right. Cleo is about to polish off that monster. This dream space is growing unstable. What's left to do?"

"Mal has suggested we leave the bound sorcerer here for a taste of his own dish," said Jacob placidly. "I am about to suggest that, tempting as such a revenge may sound, it's unwise. While he will almost certainly die under these circumstances, there's a small chance he will find a way to wake. Dark sorcerers who survive failed executions come back craftier and harder to kill. We can't simply cut his head off, either. He'll only wake up. I suggest we wipe his mind. Make him forget everything. Even how to breathe. He'll die at once, and there will be no uncertainty." He glanced at Mal. "This may seem less satisfying, but we'll all sleep better knowing this won't happen again."

"Jessica?" asked Azrael. She'd been trapped in the void. She deserved a say in what happened here.

Jessica took a deep breath. "What Jacob said."

Mal made a face. "Fine, fine."

On the other side of the fountain, Cleo had gotten a death grip on the snake's throat. It lashed furiously, but it was already dissolving, running over the ground like hot tar. Beyond the flagstones, the hedge looked translucent. The dream world was growing foggier.

A face appeared in the circle of light high overhead—a human face with red hair, haloed against the brilliant sky of the real world.

Jessica broke into a grin. "Tod!"

Azrael smiled up at him as well. "Glad to see you awake!"

Tod was panting. Azrael guessed he'd run all the way from the distant suite over the library. He also noted that Tod was wearing what looked like one of Azrael's shirts. *What else was he supposed to wear?*

"Can I help?" he shouted down at them.

"Get a ladder!" called Amos.

Everyone looked at him in surprise. The lemur flicked his tail. "Why waste magic? You're about to use a bunch of it sending this fellow down the river."

Loudain nodded. "What will it be, Azrael? You and your people have suffered. It's your call. I doubt this sorcerer will escape if you leave him here, but Jacob is right. I prefer quick and certain executions."

"I'll kill him," said Azrael quietly. "Jessica, I need my coat for a moment." He reached into an inner pocket and took out a folded memory charm. Azrael whispered more runes into it, shaping the spell, making it more powerful, more complete, ultimately deadly. At last, he said, "Nicholas Horatio Holloway, look at me."

Nicholas raised his head.

"Get up," said Azrael.

He tried. He really did, but the binding spell was making him unsteady—a common side effect. *Die on your knees, then.* "Do you have anything to say for yourself?" asked Azrael.

Nicholas shook his head, his expression stony.

"Did you attempt to murder the High Mage Council, along with my friends and associates?"

He was bound. He could not lie. "Yes."

"Were any other humans involved in your plot?"

"No."

"Is anyone depending on you for food or shelter? A child, a parent, a stray cat? Anyone at all?" Azrael did not intend to make the same mistake as the High Council. "If you have innocent dependents, we will see that they do not suffer."

Nicholas shook his head.

Azrael was tempted to ask for a detailed explanation of the magic Nicholas had used, but the dream was collapsing. Time was running out, and Azrael was finding this whole process increasingly distasteful. He reminded himself of Mal's panic and despair on the beach, Jessica waiting forever in the dream of a burned out theater, lonely and confused. He remembered Lucy's lost expression of only a few moments ago. *She had better be alright.*

Azrael crouched in front of his enemy. Nicholas eyed the glowing ball, his face slack and empty. "How did you do it?" he whispered. "How did you break the memory charm?"

"I have friends," said Azrael. *Friends who fought for me, friends who believed in me, friends who wrestled me to the ground when they had to.*

Nicholas nodded, eyes still on the deadly light. "You don't have to choke me with it. I'll just open my mouth."

He knows he needs to swallow it. In spite of himself, Azrael thought, *What a waste of knowledge and talent.* The spell's light illuminated the sorcerer's tangled hair, scruffy beard, and acne. It glinted in his dark, hollow eyes. "I have friends," Azrael heard himself say again. "But you don't, do you?"

Nicholas shook his head. "Guess that makes the difference, huh?" His eyes flicked to Azrael's face and he tried to smile.

"And I'm nobody, and I guess they call you Azrael of the Shroud for a reason. Come on, Professor, I'm gonna lose my nerve and start thrashing if you don't feed me that thing and get this over with." Under his breath, he muttered, "Gods, just let it be over."

"How old are you?"

"Fifteen."

A memory: *I escaped alone from Polois. I have been alone all my life. That is true. That is a foundational truth.*

Except it isn't. Because I didn't. There was someone else. There has always been someone else.

"Azrael..." Jacob spoke in a warning voice. "It is unwise to have prolonged conversations with dark sorcerers. They are manipulative."

Jessica sniffled. "He's been living on potatoes," she whispered.

"I don't see what that has to do with anything," began Lady S.

Azrael stood. "You said it was up to me."

"You can't be serious," drawled Amos. "Weren't you ready to kill us all an hour ago when you thought we might have had something to do with this?"

Mal was simply confused. "Are we going to leave him in the void after all?"

Loudain said nothing, just watched.

Azrael closed his hands, and the ball of light winked out. "I'm not going to kill him."

Nicholas blinked. He looked just as surprised as everyone else. "Why not?" said Jacob and Lady S at the same time.

"Because he's *me*," spat Azrael. "He's me without Mal."

Mal, who looked like he was on the verge of saying something harsh, shut his mouth abruptly.

"I was almost this kid," continued Azrael. *I could have been taken in by someone like Zersic so easily. I would have made the perfect apprentice to someone like that. And after Polois...* "I would have been this kid if not for Mal. But I wouldn't have Mal any more without Jessica. And I don't think either of them would have survived without Lucy and Tod."

Jacob opened his mouth, but Azrael stabbed a finger at him. "*You* would be inside that snake right now without my friends, Jacob. Because it wasn't my great skill that broke this trap. It was the people who care about me."

When Lady S spoke again, her voice had softened, "Azrael—"

"I will take responsibility for Nicholas," he said.

Loudain spoke at last. "You can't just make him a courtier. He's not—"

"Just a werewolf?" finished Azrael with a tight smile.

"He's a dark sorcerer!" objected Lady S.

"He won't be a dark sorcerer under me," said Azrael. "He does have to be an apprentice. He needs oversight and training. I realize that. However, I will keep him bound until he can be trusted. As you know, I am very good at binding and at wards."

Jacob did not look entirely convinced. Azrael gestured at Mal. "I kept *him* under control for twenty-three years until he was safe. You really think I can't handle a human boy?"

Jacob relaxed a fraction. "I take your point. Would you be offended if I checked on the two of you from time to time?"

"Not at all. I think that would make Lucy happy as well."

Loudain turned a slow, amused look on Jacob, who coughed and said quickly, "Well, then, I suggest we get out of here before we're caught in a dream void."

Nicholas was staring between them wide-eyed. He had not looked half so rattled by the threat of execution. Azrael turned to him again. "We have to go find your body, kid. We'll use gates. It shouldn't take more than a few hours, a day at most. While we're looking, I *am* going to leave you in the void. If I let you wake up, you may run. I won't risk that. Besides, you did do this to other people. You ought to know what it feels like."

Nicholas swallowed and didn't say anything.

"Waiting in the void is difficult," continued Azrael. "At some point, you'll probably think that I've changed my mind and left you here to die. I haven't, and I won't. Remember that."

Nicholas spoke in a sudden rush, "I'm in a locked cellar inside a burned out building that's mostly collapsed. It's locked from the inside. I don't know if you can find me. The whole valley is a wasteland since…since the council burned the circus. They left spell traps. It's hard to move around. If you've got magic, I mean."

"Is it like in the dream?" asked Jessica gently. "Is the cellar in the same place?"

Nicholas blinked at her. "Yes, only everything is more burned in real life. I made sure the dream had landmarks still standing. I could use it to move around and find some of the spell traps without setting them off."

"I think I can still find the cellar," said Jessica. "Is there really nothing to eat but potatoes?"

Nicholas gave a miserable laugh. "I am running out of those. Even if you let me wake up, I'll probably starve. Or die in a spell trap."

"I'll find you," said Jessica. "Or Tod will."

"Tod is the wolf?" asked Nicholas.

"Yes."

"I thought he was a night terror. The dream was lousy with them for a while."

Cleo came sauntering up to them, looking like a human child again, disturbingly covered in blood. She was licking it off her fingers. "You throw a good party, Boss. Heya, Mal. You want a taste of this?"

Mal made a face. "Dark magic. Ew."

Cleo shrugged. "Your loss."

Azrael shook his head. "Thank you, Cleo. You are dismissed to the astral plane. Run along home."

She gave him a huge, bloody grin and waved. "Always a pleasure, Lord Azrael!" Then she was gone.

Tod had found a ladder, and the others were already ascending as the fog thickened and the fountain disappeared. Azrael climbed up last. He looked back once and saw Nicholas still kneeling on the fading ground. He looked small and alone on the vanishing pavers in the drifting mist. Their eyes met, and Azrael could see his fear, but also something else. *He doesn't know if he can trust me, but he wants to. That's a good sign, I think. A good start.*

49

Jessica

Two days later, Jessica walked into the grand ballroom of the Shrouded Isle for an impromptu Midnight Revel. It had been hastily prepared, announced only that morning. Azrael did not usually hold Revels so close together, and not all the courtiers had chosen to attend. However, Jessica estimated she was looking at a couple hundred sparkling people mingling under the soft lights.

The weather had gotten abruptly cooler—more winter than fall. Jessica wore a red velvet dress, elbow-length black gloves, and the black boots from last time. The dress had a low back and a full skirt. Her lips were red, her golden hair piled on top of her head. She'd chosen a mask made entirely of stiff, black lace.

Yuli had come with her. She hadn't wanted to, but Jessica had insisted. "You need to leave your room. I'm sorry I wasn't here for you earlier. Please come out and see people."

"Was it Mal?" asked Yuli. "Did he kidnap you, Jessica?"

"No. We were both kidnapped. It's a long story. I'll tell you someday, but let's just have fun this evening."

And they did. They danced with each other and with other people. They drank colorful cocktails and played dominoes as the atmosphere in the room grew more lively. Yuli was laughing more, smiling. She'd chosen a black satin dress, which Jessica thought looked too much like mourning, but she had to admit that Yuli made mourning look sexy.

"Are you still planning to open your bookstore after you leave here?" asked Jessica.

Yuli shrugged. "Yeah, I guess. Maybe with someone other than Terrance. Or maybe by myself. I don't know."

"Tod said you helped him find me."

"Did I? That's good. He just wanted envelopes from your letters. I guess he can use magic. I was in the middle of bawling my eyes out, and I sort of…embarrassed myself."

Jessica laughed. "How?"

"I said you should have chosen him instead of Mal."

Jessica nearly choked on her drink.

"I know, I know!" exclaimed Yuli, "but he surprised me, and I was sitting in a pile of tissues, and he was really nice about it, and I said something stupid. Now I feel like an idiot. I'm sorry you and Mal had to go through…whatever happened to you."

Jessica smiled into her drink. "You should ask Tod to dance."

Yuli shook her head. "He's the kind of guy who is nice to everyone, but he only really likes a few people. I'm not one of them. He's really nice, though."

"And hot," said Jessica with a smirk. "Nice to watch him coming *and* going."

Yuli laughed nervously. "He lives here. He probably only wants to be friends with other people who live here."

"You should ask him to dance," repeated Jessica.

"I haven't even seen him tonight."

Jessica, who'd been watching Tod dance for the last five minutes, gestured with her drink. "Right there."

Yuli squinted. "Oh."

Jessica plopped another drink in front of her. "For courage!"

"Jessica…"

"Drink it. And then go over there."

And Jessica did something she hadn't tried before—not on someone she didn't personally intend to seduce. She gently and deliberately lowered Yuli's inhibitions. *This is how a succubus tries to make you feel better, my friend. At least I know Tod will be nice about it.*

Yuli took a deep breath, stood up, and walked across the dance floor. Tod looked surprised when she tapped him on the shoulder, but not unhappy. A moment later, they were moving together. Two minutes later, they were talking and laughing.

Jessica watched with a sense of satisfaction. She let her eyes drift over the beautiful frescoes, the stately columns, garden torches and the sparkle of the pool beyond. *I'll have to ask Tod what it was like to grow up here. Obviously, a child would need to stay out of adult areas, but I think it could be really wonderful.*

She was so lost in thought that she didn't see Mal until he slid onto the couch beside her. "You know what those black gloves and black boots look like?"

Jessica rolled her eyes.

Mal put an arm around her and kissed the side of her neck. "Foxy lady."

Jessica shook her head. "It's so much harder and stranger than I thought."

"I could tell a dick joke right now."

"I think you just did."

"I assume you're talking about shapeshifting?"

"Yes, you make it look easy, but it isn't."

Mal shrugged. "I'm a five-dimensional creature. If I don't change shape now and then, I feel cramped."

Jessica leaned back against his shoulder, and he pulled her close, his thumb absently stroking the side of her breast. She could smell the clean scent of his skin and hair, feel his warmth. "Did Azrael get his magical airlock finished?"

"Yep. Two hours ago. The other magicians helped. We're ready for the rest of those nosy assholes to show up tomorrow, I guess." He yawned.

Jessica smiled. "Sleepy incubus."

Mal grunted. This party was intended for him to recharge, but Jessica could tell he was tired from more than the use of his magic. His ordeal in the dream world had taken something out of him.

I suppose it took something out of me, too. Jessica felt as though she could curl up against him and go to sleep right here. *This may be the most subdued Revel ever.* "I'm so glad we're here," she whispered.

"Me, too."

Someone cleared his throat, and Jessica looked up to see a slender man in a tuxedo standing beside their couch. His mask was black and white porcelain. The light was shining at his back, and it took Jessica an instant to recognize him. "Ren!" She bounced to her feet.

Mal scrambled up behind her. "You came!"

Azrael looked a little nervous. "Actually, I brought my guests. They...um...wanted to see what these parties looked like. I think they actually want to make sure nobody's being abused."

"Well, I do hope they'll stay for the full experience," purred Mal. "I would love to see Jacob loosen up a bit."

Jessica rolled her eyes. "They're magicians, Mal. I'm sure they're warded."

"So is he," said Mal with a nod at Azrael. "But I bet I get him to put some grass-stains on that tux by the end of the night anyway."

Azrael swallowed. Jessica could tell he was worried about being humiliated in front of his guests. She put her arms around him and laid her cheek on his shoulder. "I'm so glad you came," she whispered. "Mal will be gentle."

Mal put his arms around both of them. Jessica felt profoundly content.

"I see you got the brat out of the garden," said Mal into Azrael's hair.

Azrael laughed. "Not without effort. He didn't actually want to attend the Revel. He just wanted to keep working."

"I think that qualifies him as a dark sorcerer right there," said Mal.

"I think he's a little young for your parties," said Jessica.

"And he is warded," continued Azrael. "You will not be feeding on him or any other magician without my permission."

Mal harrumphed. He had accepted Azrael's decision about Nicholas, but Jessica thought it would be a while before Mal forgave him. For his part, Nicholas's brief possession had clearly left him terrified of Mal. Jessica thought that was probably for the best.

Azrael's first assignment for his new apprentice had been shoring up the weak place in the garden left by the dream gate. "If I have an incursion of night terrors, faeries, or chimeras, you will be cleaning privies for a while," Azrael had told him.

Nicholas certainly wasn't allergic to work. He'd spent his first day in the garden from sunrise to sunset, stopping only to wolf down food as though he'd never seen any before. He clearly had no idea how to behave among all the glittering people or what to think of the sensuous atmosphere. But he knew how to work. Jessica suspected that he and Azrael would get along very well after everything quieted down.

Jessica lifted her face to her lovers. She spoke cautiously, "The westernmost of the Provinces allows multiple marriages."

Azrael smiled. "I was wondering whether you knew about that. One of the island kingdoms will also perform them."

"Can we?" she asked breathlessly.

"Of course."

"Oh!" Jessica wanted to bounce, but she had too many arms around her. "Will you help me pick out a dress?"

Azrael looked sheepish. "I already have a number of possible—"

Jessica laughed out loud. "You already have. Of course you already have."

"No, no, I just have some ideas."

"Can I wear something interesting?" asked Mal.

Azrael's eyes flicked to his face with a twinkle. "You want me to dress you up like a doll?"

"Yes. Because you look at me like you want to eat me."

Azrael's smile lifted his mask at the edges. He glanced at Jessica. "What are you going to tell your family?"

"The truth. My parents, at least. Possibly my siblings, too."

"Do you think they'll respond well?"

Jessica shrugged. "My parents were in a triad with an incubus for years. That's how I came to be. I think they'll be upset with themselves for putting me in danger by not realizing what I am. I can't imagine that they'll have a problem with the three of us. It runs in the family, apparently."

Azrael was looking at her in astonishment. "I...I think I would like to meet your parents."

Jessica was glad to hear it. "Also," she continued, "I am going to tell them your concerns about my middle name. If they agree, you can make them forget it, perhaps replace it with something else. But not without their consent."

"That seems fair." Azrael looked uncomfortable. "I realize that was not my unilateral decision to make. I apologize."

Jessica kissed him on the cheek.

Mal squeezed them both. "Is Lucy here?"

"She's with Jacob. Please don't pick a fight, Mal."

"I won't. I just wanted to talk to her for a moment."

Azrael disengaged from their arms and straightened his bow tie. "I should go back over there."

Jessica looped one arm through Azrael's and one arm through Mal's and they walked together through the throng of happy people. *I am so proud of you,* she thought. *I am so proud of you both.*

50

Mal

The magicians were not difficult to spot. They were the only people in the room not wearing masks. They sat at a table a little apart from the main flow of activity, watching and talking to each other. As Mal approached, he noticed one person he didn't recognize—a short, stocky man with a curly mass of blond beard and twinkling, mischievous eyes. He was sitting beside Lady S, drinking and chatting, but it wasn't until

Mal caught the flash of silver under the edge of his shirt collar that he recognized him. "Amos."

The demon raised his glass. "You throw a good party, Mal. Gods know we needed a cooldown after all that nonsense with the airlock."

Mal grinned. "I doubt you'll find anything to feed on here. People do tend to stay busy at my parties."

Amos chuckled. "Touché. S owns a spa. It's worth a visit. It doesn't preclude getting busy, but it's not quite the same energy."

Mal grinned. "I came over here to talk to Lucy." He finally spotted her, leaning around Jacob to say something to Azrael. Lucy was dressed in her white gown and mink half-cape, a string of pearls around her neck and gold flashing in her ears. Her eyeshadow and lipstick were flawless. She looked cool and unapproachable, and more than a little draconic. Her glance passed right through Mal.

"Amos!" exclaimed Jessica. "I did not recognize you. Did I hear that you and Lady S own a spa?"

Amos and Lady S launched into a description of their little empire of decadence. Mal had no doubt that Jessica would soon have a standing invitation.

He left her to it and walked around the table. "Lucy?" She was sitting between Azrael and Jacob now, and she looked up with an expression that wasn't entirely friendly. Mal had a vivid memory of her last visit to a Revel. He held up his hands. "I'm not here to fight. I just wanted a dance."

Lucy looked skeptical. "I think you and I have already had one dance too many."

"Please?"

Lucy sighed. She got up. "Back in a moment, gentlemen. Try not to kill each other."

"I was going to say the same to you," returned Azrael.

Mal smiled. Lucy tossed her head.

The music was slow and sensuous. Lucy put one hand in Mal's and the other on his shoulder, but she kept a few inches between them. He could tell she was waiting to see whether he would take liberties. *Surely you don't suppose I think permission once is permission forever?*

He felt a moment's irritation, a desire to defend himself or disagree with her before she'd said a word. But then he thought about spending eighty years alone in a spirit vessel. And he stifled his impulse.

They moved around the floor for a few moments in silence amid the beautiful music and the flirting courtiers. Lucy relaxed a little. Mal spoke at last. "Thank you for saving my life."

Lucy nodded.

"When you came to the Revel last time," continued Mal, "you just wanted to see whether it was a place you'd be comfortable with Jacob, didn't you?"

Another nod.

"I'm sorry I picked a fight. I'm sorry I do it all the time. I don't want to fight with you anymore."

Lucy sighed. "It's not entirely your fault, Mal." She hesitated, a note of wry humor in her voice. "I mean, it's mostly your fault."

He laughed.

"I used to hope that you'd get weaker," continued Lucy softly, "staying on the mortal plane for so long... I kept testing you."

He was shocked to hear her admit this out loud.

Lucy shrugged. "I'm really not very good at losing, that's all."

Mal reached down and tilted her chin up to look him in the face. "Malcharius Thardarian Vi'aesha Charn."

Lucy's pupils dilated. Her mouth opened soundlessly.

"So you always have a trump card," continued Mal. "So you never feel like I can just shove you out of the way. You win."

Lucy blinked and lowered her face suddenly. Her dancing faltered. After an instant's hesitation, Mal pulled her against him. She put her head on his chest without the slightest resistance. She didn't say anything for the longest time. At last, Mal said, "Lucy?"

She took a breath. Mal felt it hitch. He realized that he'd never seen Lucy cry. Not in all the years he'd known her.

"You could have asked for anything," he whispered. "You could have named your price for saving me. I was so desperate and so scared. But you didn't. You saved me, and you taught me to cloak, and that saved all of us in the end. You can act as cold about it as you like, but I know—"

Lucy raised her head. She had tear tracks in her mascara. "Shhh, dove. Shhh." They were just holding each other now, moving with the music. Lucy swallowed. "I would never use a name, willingly given in friendship, to hurt someone. You know that, right?"

"You can if you want to."

Lucy shook her head. "Let's just say we both win. And I don't want to fight with you anymore, either." Lucy tucked her head against his chest and they danced for a moment in silence.

At last, the music changed to something more lively. The lights came up. Mal got a look at the corner where the magicians were sitting. He was amused to see Jessica still talking to Lady S and Amos, while Azrael, Jacob, and Loudain appeared to be engaged in a lively discussion, illustrated with empty drink cups. Azrael was gesticulating as he talked. Jacob was drawing in the air with magic. Loudain was laughing so hard his face had turned as red as his beard.

Lucy followed Mal's gaze. "My gods. Are they telling war stories?"

"That's what it looks like," said Mal.

"*Our* Azrael, drinking with peers and socializing in a convivial manner? Are you sure he's not still possessed?"

Mal shrugged. "You and I are cuddling on the dance floor."

"You're right," agreed Lucy. "We have all lost our minds."

"Looks like a good story," said Mal. "You want to go back and cuddle with Jacob?"

Lucy nodded.

"You, um, might want to fix your mascara first."

"Oh, gods." She dropped her face in embarrassment, and Mal leaned down to kiss her on the cheek. "You are so pretty, Lucy."

He could feel the alien tingle of her magic. When she looked up again, there wasn't a smudge out of place. "Thank you."

"You're welcome. Have fun at my party."

Lucy left him and strolled back across the room. Jacob looked more than a little surprised when she sat down in his lap, but he was quick to put an arm around her. Lucy slid an arm across his shoulders, somehow still poised and elegant. A moment later, she joined in the conversation. Mal had no doubt that she had more war stories than all of them.

And I want to listen. But first... He'd spotted Tod, sitting on a couch where people often waited for someone to return from the washroom. *This won't take long.*

"I'm not actually alone," said Tod when Mal joined him.

"I didn't think you were." Mal leaned back and closed his eyes. "I heard you climbed into our bed naked, pinned Azrael down, and put cuffs on him."

Tod gave a startled grunt of laughter. "Not my idea."

Mal grinned without opening his eyes. "Don't worry; he likes it."

Another nervous laugh. "Not from me he didn't." Under his breath, Tod added, "Never been so scared in my life. I think he was about to pull my lungs out through my ears."

Mal took a deep breath. "I was talking to Jessica about you."

"I wish you wouldn't."

"I mean, about what happened before."

Tod sighed. "That was years ago, Mal. Can we talk about this another time? I really am waiting for someone."

"I thought," continued Mal, "that you were one of those people who want me all to themselves. We fuck once or twice, and they start following me around and acting jealous and begging for my attention, and I don't understand, and it's really annoying."

Tod said nothing.

"But I was talking to Jessica, and I realized that maybe that wasn't it at all. You live here, and I live here, and maybe you just wanted a friend who wouldn't leave. And I was an asshole about it."

Tod buried his face in his hands. "It was a long time ago, Mal. I *did* think I was in love with you. And I was lonely and I didn't understand what you were. I did want a friend..." He drew a deep breath. "I got over it."

Mal swallowed. "Tod, I'm barely human."

"I know."

"I didn't understand. I didn't know much about friends. Forgive me?"

"I already did."

"When Jessica and I were traveling, I'd go hunting as a panther sometimes. I thought about going around here." He leaned over to speak in a conspiratorial whisper, "I like to chase Azrael's ornamental carp, but he gets mad, so I thought maybe I should go looking for rabbits instead."

Tod laughed in spite of himself.

Mal leaned back, grinning. "Come with me? On four legs?"

Tod looked uncertain.

"Jessica might come, but she doesn't like to see anything killed, not even a mouse. I doubt that'll change just because she's a fox. But maybe. Come chase rabbits with me? Or with us?"

Tod smiled. "I'll think about it."

At that moment, Jessica's friend Yuli came walking towards them. "Is that who you're waiting on?" asked Mal.

"Yes. She doesn't like you much."

"I know. I never understood why."

"It is a mystery how anyone could dislike you," said Tod with a smirk.

Yuli stopped in front of them, her full, pink lips pulled down in a frown.

"Yuli, Mal," said Tod. "Mal, Yuli."

"We've met," said Yuli.

"Not really," said Mal.

"I think you're kind of an asshole," said Yuli.

"I am," agreed Mal.

That brought a surprised smile. "But you make Jessica happy," she continued. "As long as that's true, you're alright. Do you want to play dominoes, Tod? I suppose Mal can play, too."

"Thank you." Mal stood up. "But some people are telling stories that I'd like to hear. Have a good time at the party."

Epilogue: Six Months Later

Azrael

Azrael leaned against the smooth stone lip of a private hot spring, feeling as relaxed as he'd ever felt in his life. A breeze blew through the large, open windows, smelling of mountain air, earth, and pine. He could see a patch of blue sky. Mal and Jessica's voices carried to him faintly on the wind: Mal's rumble, Jessica's singing laugh, a comforting background of peace and contentment.

They came through the door behind him a moment later. Azrael could tell they were both in animal form by the scrabble involved in opening the door. Jessica's claws went *click, click, click* on the stone. She changed as she reached him and sat down on the edge of the pool, naked and breathless, dangling her feet in the warm water. "It's *so* beautiful, Ren. We ran down one of the trails all the way to the lake. There are flowers everywhere. The water is cool if we want a different kind of swim."

Mal, who had not changed shape, stretched out on the stone and rested his head beside Azrael's shoulder opposite Jessica. He licked Azrael's ear and the side of his neck, making him shiver in spite of the warmth. "There is sushi for dinner," he said between licks. "I have never eaten sushi, but it smells divine. I'm glad we came here instead of a pocket world. Amos is a genius, and Lady S is an artist."

Jessica kicked her feet in the water. "I agree. I'm glad we came to a real place for our honeymoon. Even though a book wouldn't age or change...sometimes real things are better. We'll age and change, and so will this place. I love it."

"You should get out and get ready for dinner," said Mal against Azrael's ear. His whiskers tickled. Azrael reached up to stroke his velvet head before rising from the water.

He grabbed a fluffy towel and dried himself off. He started to wrap it around his waist, then shrugged and threw it in the hamper before strolling out of the hot spring bath into the private garden of the honeymoon suite. The early summer air was a perfect temperature for nakedness. Purple, blue, and yellow flowers grew in a riot around the bathhouse and along the walk up to the cottage.

Even beyond the garden wall, there were no other suites in sight. The spa was located high in the mountains of Zolsestron, with cottages set well apart along a series of trails. This was the area from which Azrael originated, although he'd never been back since those fearful days when he and Mal had fled through these mountains in thigh-deep winter snow. It was strange to see faces like his own among the staff and in the villages—pale skin, dark hair, almond eyes. The smells of the woods and even of the food brought back complex feelings and memories.

Azrael had only walked through the cottage briefly on his way to the hot spring when they arrived. He came into the bedroom for the first time now and found it predictably lovely—an enormous bed with a velvety red comforter, chocolate and roses on the pillows, a dish of oil, a bottle of wine on ice, their travel trunks neatly laid out on stands. The windows were large and open, but they looked out on the walled garden. The room was utterly private, but full of summer air and light. Lush paintings of flowers hung on the walls—blues and greens and golds, color everywhere.

Jessica gave a sigh of pleasure and went to put the roses in the vase provided. "Glass of wine?" she asked.

"Certainly." Azrael went to his trunk and began selecting clothes.

Jessica uncorked the bottle. She poured three glasses and stood in front of the window, her golden skin radiant in the summer light, her glossy hair blowing in the wind, her breasts a soft curve in silhouette.

"I got a letter right before we left," said Jessica without turning around. "It came to my parents and they debated about giving it to me. It's from my father. My incubus father."

"Oh." Azrael's fingers paused on his dress shirt.

"He's living in the mundane world," said Jessica. "He killed someone by accident. He swears it was an accident, and my parents believe him. But the fallout was very bad, and he took himself away from the Shattered Sea."

Mal was standing beside Azrael, still a panther. "That's a significant sacrifice. Living without magic… It would kill an astral demon. It would be difficult even for an earthborn demon."

Jessica nodded. "My parents say he's a good person. They really loved him. They didn't know where he was for years, and there's no return address on the letter even now. I think they would have followed him if they'd been able, but he didn't want them to. They think he was trying to protect them." Jessica sipped her wine.

"Does he want to come see you?" asked Azrael.

Jessica nodded. "What do you think?"

"I would be happy to host him on the Shrouded Isle. Your parents, too, if they like. Mal and I could tell you if he's a liar."

Jessica turned away from the window, her face relaxing. "I'd like that."

"If he's even a little bit like you, he can't be bad," said Mal.

Jessica smiled at him fondly.

"They should come this summer before the students arrive in fall," continued Mal. "I'm sure we'll have our hands full once that happens."

"There are only ten in this first class," said Azrael mildly.

"Ten warded magicians that I can't feed on wandering around my island," growled Mal. "I always thought one was too many."

"They will not be wandering," said Azrael firmly. "They will stay strictly in their area."

"Have you decided whether Nicholas will be among them?" asked Jessica.

Azrael shook his head. "Apprentice is a more advanced role." His mouth twitched up. "I may make him the janitor for the school, though."

Mal rumbled a laugh. Jessica raised her eyebrows.

"It's an important job," continued Azrael, "in a magical school. I'll make sure nobody abuses him."

Jessica nodded. "It would be good for him to make some friends among the other students. Right now, he's still feeling pretty bitter towards other magicians."

"Except this one." Mal rubbed his head against Azrael's hip in a feline kiss.

"Agreed. He thinks his teacher hung the moon."

Azrael looked uncomfortable. "Mostly he thinks I decided not to kill him."

Mal shook his head. "Jessica is right. He doesn't much like the rest of us, but he thinks you're amazing. You are."

"Good father material," said Jessica with a grin.

Azrael laughed.

Mal rubbed against his hip again. "I think we should do one other thing before dinner."

Azrael looked down at him with a trace of amusement. "You know the reason I kept you as a panther for so many years is that I was trying *not* to feel attracted to you. I really don't want to have sex with a panther."

"I know, but I want to do one thing you don't usually let me do. Please?"

Azrael swallowed. "What?"

Mal stepped behind him. Azrael felt his warm tongue on the small of his back, then lower. "Mal…"

"You are as clean as clean can be," purred Mal. "There is nothing to be embarrassed about. Let me?"

"I…" Azrael swallowed. His face was on fire. Mal's muscular tongue pressed between his ass cheeks and Azrael let out his breath in a hiss. Warm, wet licking. Azrael suddenly did not trust his legs and leaned forward against the trunk.

Then Jessica was in front of him, giggling, turning him into her arms. She kissed him while Mal's tongue lapped over his balls and asshole. There did not seem to be enough air in the room. He was going to fall over. Jessica stroked his cock, and his arms closed around her reflexively.

She sucked his earlobe and murmured, "We should practice baby-making sex!"

"That's what I thought," said Mal between licks.

Azrael felt dizzy. "Is this how babies are made? I know even less about it than I imagined. Oh gods, Mal."

He was purring, creating vibrations that went all the way to Azrael's crotch. Jessica's thumb ran over the head of his cock, and a spasm shuddered through him that was very close to climax. Azrael made a choking nose. "Slow down. Mal, Jessica, please. Slow down."

"I'm not even using magic," murmured Mal.

Azrael removed one hand from around Jessica's shoulders and slid it between her legs. She whimpered into his mouth, and her hand on his cock faltered.

She was already wet. Soon she was wetter. He found her clit and rubbed and circled until she gently pushed his hand away. Jessica guided his cock inside her—just the head; they were at the wrong angle for anything else, but she felt hot and slick and tantalizing. She brought his thumb back to her clit, and he stroked while she pressed herself against him, one leg wrapping around his waist, leaning.

"I'm going to fall over," panted Azrael. "I can't… Mal, that's…"

"Good?" purred Mal.

"Yes, yes! Fuck!"

Mal stepped away from him. In spite of his own objections, Azrael wanted to beg him to come back. Then big, warm hands grasped his hips. *Oh, yes, please. Please, please, please.*

Jessica was already standing with the backs of her legs against the bed. Mal pushed, and she tipped over with Azrael on top of her. His cock slid all the way inside her sweet, tight warmth. Jessica made a low noise, panting. Azrael paused, gritting his teeth, trying not to come.

Mal's fingers pressed inside him, slick with oil from the dish on the bedside table. Mal bent his head over Azrael's shoulder and Jessica leaned up to kiss him. "Such a sweet incubus," she murmured. Mal's curls brushed against Azrael's face. Then his hot mouth met the side of Azrael's neck, licking, sucking, and nibbling. His hands settled on Azrael's hips, his cock pushing.

I want you inside me. I want you both. I want you everywhere. Azrael whispered a rune and took down his wards. His body lit up with blue light just as Mal's cock pressed inside him.

Mal growled his pleasure into Azrael's ear. The sensation of penetration was overwhelming. Mal began to thrust, rocking all three of them. Both demons were pulling on Azrael's magic, pulling on each other, pulling *through* him. Jessica panted into Azrael's ear, murmuring, pleading, whimpering. She wrapped her legs around them both.

Mal picked up speed. At last, he pressed Azrael deep inside Jessica and pulled so hard on their magic that Azrael could not have held back the orgasm if his life had depended on it. Pleasure shuddered through him, clenching his balls, his asshole, his whole body. Jessica made a high-pitched cry against his ear. Mal thrust one more time and sent a ripple of magic through them like a gift. A different kind of pleasure flooded Azrael's senses—warm in his belly, an intense sense of belonging and delight.

Mal backed off of him slowly. Then peeled Azrael off of Jessica. They flopped down side by side in the enormous bed, struggling for breath. "See?" said Mal when he could speak again. "Baby-making sex."

"Totally," agreed Jessica.

Azrael laughed. "I doubt that's in any marriage manual."

"I mean," continued Mal airily. "It's not my *only* idea. We can try some others."

Jessica rolled over and kissed him. Azrael managed to make his arms and legs work well enough to put his head on Mal's chest. Mal stroked his hair. After a while, Mal said, "Sushi is like eating ornamental carp, right?"

Azrael and Jessica both said, "No," together.

Then they got up and got dressed and showed him. Later, after they'd had wine and dinner and another dip in the hot spring, after they'd made love again and read for an hour and turned out the lights, Azrael settled his hand in Jessica's. Mal was already asleep with his head on Azrael's chest, breathing softly. Jessica's sleepy fingers threaded through Azrael's. "Perfect day," he whispered.

"Perfect," she agreed. "And we're going to have so many more."

About the Author

A. H. Lee is a medical professional. She also writes epic fantasy under Abigail Hilton. You can contact her at abigail.hilton@pavoninebooks.com. She also has a facebook author page for A. H. Lee: https://www.facebook.com/AHLeeAuthor/

Printed in Great Britain
by Amazon

14849785R00148